Praise for *The Emperor's Babe*

"A vividly imagined albeit distinctly modern look at a woman's role in Roman times by a talented writer with a fertile mind and a playful spirit." —*Publishers Weekly*

"Evaristo . . . has written the novel in springy, street-smart verse that swings between sour-apple satire, sweet-corn sentiment and, from time to time, lines of piercing lyricism. What the verse does is oddly similar to what drawings do in graphic novels: . . . They seem to project a backlighting, a resonance in perspective, upon the heads-on words of the narration."

—Richard Eder, *The New York Times*

"Irreverent, fun, and amusingly anachronistic . . . The . . . gladiatorial battle [scene] is not to be missed. . . . Consistently amusing, clever, and inventive." —*Library Journal* (starred review)

"Evaristo's triumph is to transmute politics and history into a glittering fiction whose words leap off the page into life. Anarchic, she calls it, but brilliant would do just as well."

—*The Times* (London)

"Streetwise, sassy, audacious . . . a dizzy linguistic carnival . . . Evaristo is youthful and daring, with hidden depths of wisdom and hilarity, and she has delivered an entirely new concept for the historical novel." —*The Independent*

"Written in fresh, zingy, witty language that combines tags of Latin, historically authentic references and twenty-first-century teen slang, [*The Emperor's Babe*] is a fast, exciting read . . . a modern work of art that uses the literary tradition with such light assurance that everything seems new. . . . Vivat Zuleika."

—*The Sunday Times*

"Fresh and original . . . Funny, playful, erotic and ultimately tragic, Evaristo's tale has a lively, contemporary feel, while also touching on deeper themes about domination and empire."

—*The Bookseller*

"Readable, sexy, delicious . . . I loved this book!"

—Helen Dunmore

"What an exhilarating experience it is to read *The Emperor's Babe*, so fast-talking and fast-moving that it blows away the centuries between ancient and contemporary as skillfully as it explodes the borders between novel and poem. Wildly entertaining then deeply affecting, a fusion of lightness, subtlety and sensuality, it's a miracle book, one that can bring the dead back to sassy life."

—Ali Smith

ABOUT THE AUTHOR

Bernardine Evaristo was born in London to a Nigerian father and an English mother. She trained as an actress and has traveled widely. Her debut novel, *Lara,* won the EMMA (Ethnic Multicultural Media Awards) Best Book Award. A former Poet in Residence at the Museum of London, where she conducted the historical research that partly inspired *The Emperor's Babe,* Bernardine Evaristo has won an Arts Council of England Writers' Award and held writing fellowships at the University of East Anglia and Barnard College. She lives in London.

THE EMPEROR'S BABE

BERNARDINE
EVARISTO

PENGUIN BOOKS

PENGUIN BOOKS
Published by the Penguin Group
Penguin Group (USA) Inc., 375 Hudson Street,
New York, New York 10014, U.S.A.
Penguin Books Ltd, 80 Strand, London WC2R 0RL, England
Penguin Books Australia Ltd, 250 Camberwell Road,
Camberwell, Victoria 3124, Australia
Penguin Books Canada Ltd, 10 Alcorn Avenue,
Toronto, Ontario, Canada M4V 3B2
Penguin Books India (P) Ltd, 11 Community Centre,
Panchsheel Park, New Delhi – 110 017, India
Penguin Books (N.Z.) Ltd, Cnr Rosedale and Airborne Roads,
Albany, Auckland, New Zealand
Penguin Books (South Africa) (Pty) Ltd, 24 Sturdee Avenue,
Rosebank, Johannesburg 2196, South Africa

Penguin Books Ltd, Registered Offices:
80 Strand, London WC2R 0RL, England

First published in Great Britain by Hamish Hamilton Ltd 2001
First published in the United States of America by Viking Penguin,
a member of Penguin Putnam Inc. 2002
Published in Penguin Books 2004

ISBN 0-670-03071-6 (hc.)
ISBN 0 14 20.0171 6 (pbk.)
CIP data available

147468846

For my father,
Julius Taiwo Obayomi Evaristo: 1927-2001

The one duty we owe to history is to rewrite it.

—OSCAR WILDE

CONTENTS

THE EMPEROR'S BABE

PROLOGUE

AMO AMAS AMAT

Who do you love? Who *do* you love,
when the man you married goes off

for months on end, quelling rebellions
at the frontiers, or playing hot-shot senator in Rome;

his flashy villa on the Palatine Hill, home
to another woman, I hear,

one who has borne him offspring.
My days are spent roaming this house,

its vast mosaic walls full of the scenes on Olympus,
for my husband loves melodrama.

They say his mistress is an actress,
a flaxen-Fräulein type, from Germania Superior.

Oh, everyone envied me, *Illa Bella Negreeta!*
born in the back of a shop on Gracechurch Street,

who got hitched to a Roman nobleman,
whose parents sailed out of Khartoum on a barge,

no burnished throne, no poop of beaten gold,
but packed with vomiting brats

and cows releasing warm turds
on to their bare feet. Thus perfumed,

they made it to Londinium on a donkey,
with only a thin purse and a fat dream.

Here in the drizzle of this wild west town
Dad wandered the streets looking for work,

but there was no room at the inn,
so he set up shop on the kerb

and sold sweet cakes which Mum made.
(He's told me this story a mille times.)

Now he owns several shops, selling everything
from vino to shoes, veggies to tools,

and he employs all sorts to work in them,
a Syrian, Tunisian, Jew, Persian,

hopefuls just off the olive barge from Gaul,
in fact anyone who'll work for pebbles.

When Felix came after me, Dad was in ecstasy,
father-in-law to Lucius Aurelius Felix, no less.

I was spotted at the baths of Cheapside,
just budding, and my fate was sealed

by a man thrice my age and thrice my girth,
all at sweet eleven – even then Dad

thought I was getting past it.
Then I was sent off to a snooty Roman bitch

called Clarissa for decorum classes,
learnt how to talk, eat and fart,

how to get my amo amas amat right, and ditch
my second-generation plebby creole.

Zuleika accepta est.
Zuleika delicata est.
Zuleika bloody goody-two shoes est.

But I dreamt of creating mosaics,
of remaking my town with bright stones and glass.

But no! Numquam! It's not allowed.
Sure, Felix brings me presents, when he deigns

to come west. I've had Chinese silk, a marble
figurine from Turkey, gold earrings

shaped like dolphins, and I have the deepest
fondness for my husband, of course,

sort of, though he spills over me like dough
and I'm tempted to call Cook mid coitus

to come trim his sides so that he fits me.
Then it's puff and *Ciao, baby!*

Solitudoh, solitudee, solitudargh!

I

LONDINIUM TOUR GUIDE (UNOFFICIAL)

One minute it's hopscotch in bare feet,
next you're four foot up in a sedan in case

your pink stockings get dirty. No one
prepared me for marriage. Me and Alba

were the wild girls of Londinium,
sought to discover the secrets

of its hidden hearts, still too young
to withhold more than we revealed,

to join this merry cast of actors.
She was like a rag doll who'd lost its stuffing:

spiky brown hair kept short 'cos of nits;
everyone said she was either anorexic

or had worms, but Alba was so busy
chasing the dulcis vita that she just burnt

everything she ate before it turned to fat.
She'd drag me out on dangerous escapades,

we were partners in crime, banditos, renegades
she said there was more to life

than playing with friggin' dolls, like causing
trouble and discovering what grown-ups

did in private without getting caught.
We were gonna steal from the rich,

give to the poor, keep seventy-five per cent
for ourselves and live in one of them mansions

with a thousand slaves feeding us cakes,
all day every day, but until such time . . . Her dad

owned the butcher's next door but one.
Mine couldn't care less what I did.

His precious Catullus got the abacus and wax,
I got the sewing kit and tweezers.

He was *even* bought a ponytail for his curly
little head, so's he fitted in at school

with all those trendy Roman kids.
Bless his sockless feet. *Imagine.*

Some days we'd tour the tenements
of Aldersgate. He'd trail behind

like a giant sloth, his big muddy eyes
under sleepy hoods (just like his father's),

and plead with us to slow down;
I'd tell him to *futuo-off, you little runt,*

leaving him behind as we raced towards
the slums, swarming with immigrants,

freed slaves and factory workers (usual suspects).
We'd play Knock-Down-Ginger, throw stones,

break windows, then leg-it down an alley
outa-sight, arrive home breathless

and itching with flea bites and jigger-foot.
What with the alfresco sewerage running

between paving stones, now
in my neighbourhood, summer evenings

were spiced, trout fried on stalls, fresh
out of the Thames, you could eat air

or run home for supper in the back-a-yard
Dad called an atrium. That's

if the rush-hour traffic allowed, carts
clogged up the main drag to the Forum, unloading

produce from up-country or abroad.
Sometimes, I'd hear a solitary flute through an open

window, and stop . . . . breathing.
Later we'd sneak out for the vicarious thrill

of the carnal experience. Like two toms,
we'd prowl the darkened alleys, our noses

sniffing out the devastating odour of sex.
Peeping through candle-lit shutters,

we were amazed at the adult need to strip off
and stick things in each other.

Men and women, women and women,
men and men, multiples of all sorts

groaning in pain. Absolutely fascinatio!
And then we encountered death,

Lucan Africanus, the baker of Fenchurch.
I was the daughter he never had, he said

(though his eyes spelt *wife*),
gave us fresh bread dipped in honey.

Our thanks? To raid his store one night,
find his great, black, rigor mortis self

in a cloud of flour, two burnt buns for cheeks,
too much yeast in his bowels, emptied

on the floor. That stopped our missions,
for a while. Some nights we'd go to the river,

sit on the beach, look out towards
the marshy islands of Southwark,

and beyond to the jungle that was Britannia,
teeming with spirits and untamed humans.

We'd try to imagine the world beyond the city,
that country a lifetime away that Mum

called home and Dad called prison;
the city of Roma which everyone

went on about as if it were so bloody mirabilis.
We'd talk about the off-duty soldiers

who loitered in our town, everywhere,
they were everywhere, watching for lumps

on our chests, to see if our hips grew away
from our waists, always picking me out,

plucking at me in the market,
Is our little aubergine ready?

'No, I'm not, you stinking pervs,' I'd growl,
skedaddling hotfoot out of their reach.

Sometimes we'd hear grunting
on the beach and imagine some illicit

extramarital action was in progress,
we'd call out in our deepest, gruffest voices,

Hey, polizia! and rock with laughter
'cos we'd interrupted their flipping coitus,

we'd hear them tripping over themselves
as they scuffled off and then everything

changed, I got engaged. I wasn't allowed
out no more, I had to act ladylike

and Alba said it wouldn't be the same
once I'd been elevated.

THE BETRAYAL

> Time to leave your mother, dear.
> You're ready for a man.
> – HORACE

First I heard of it was overheard
when I came home unexpectedly early

from the baths 'cos it was overcrowded
and as usual they told *me* to come back later.

As I dawdled up our street, busy
with shoppers – tired of having to say *Salve!*

and *Bene, gratias* at every step to neighbours
who didn't give a toss about how I felt,

wondering if Alba could come out to play,
glad that spring was here after a long winter

when I'd had to wrap my feet in rags
or else they'd fall off –

I saw a fancy sedan parked up outside
our shop and four bronzed sedan-bearers

wearing white linen skirts with gold stripes,
leaning against the wall, waiting.

I ran the rest of the way, found the shop closed.
I heard voices, put my ear to the door.

'Sì, Mr Felix. Zuleika very obediens girl, sir.
No problemata, she make very optima wife, sir.'

'Glad to hear it, for when I saw her at the baths,
she stole my heart. Indeed,

she is so . . . exquisita, so . . . pulcherrima,
such a delicious surprise in this, shall we say,

less than dazzling little colonia.
She reminds me of the girls back in Ægyptus,

where I spent most of my teenage years,
my father was governor there, you know,

I liked the mysterious, dark ones
from the south, who would oil my limbs,

waft soundlessly around me leaving
the lingering scent of musky sandalwood

from Zanzibar in their wake.
I have been looking for a wife for some time,

and naturaliter, I wanted someone young,
someone specialis, a rare flower.'

'Sì, Mr Felix. Zuleika very specialis girl.
Yes, always at home, quietly sewing,

very placid, no back-chat.'
'Good. I have enjoyed bachelorhood

to its utmost, Anlamani, but the fiend loneliness
has become a most unwelcome friend.

I intend to make this my far-western base
and I need to warm my home with a wife.

I am a man of multiple interests: a senator,
military man, businessman, I undertake

trading missions for the government,
and I'm a landowner,

I've just bought Hertfordshire, you know.
Yet I have never been interested

in the plethora of simpering debutantes
who are paraded in the cattle-market balls

every season, mothers thrusting their powdered
wrinkled cleavages at me, supposedly

on behalf of their darling twittering daughters.
My own dear mater died young, you know,

she was so *very* benevola, I missed
her terribly when I was a boy. I still do.

Perhaps that is why it has taken me so long
to tie the knot, so to speak.

To form an attachment is to risk its loss,
is it not? I have been looking for a nice,

simplex, quiet, fidelis girl, a girl
who will not betray me with affairs,

who will not wear me out with horrid fights,
unlike my pater's subsequent three wives,

who made my life hell, *and* his,
who were of the hedonistic breed

of aristocratic matronae, determined to compete
with the husband in all spheres,

ever boastful of their sexual shenanigans,
humiliating the dear gentle man in public

and prepared to argue until dawn on matters
of politics, world affairs and the arts.

Have you heard that women now dress up
in male attire and compete in chariot races?

It has got quite out of hand in the fatherland.
Nor do I want one with cumbersome baggage.

Is my load not heavy enough?
I will of course see to an educatio for her,

and lessons in elegantia, she is of the age
where she will learn quickly.

Do not worry about her dowry, it is of no
consequentia to me, of course

you will benefit greatly from this negotium.
I think we can safely say that your business

is due to expand considerably.'
'You are very benignus gentleman, sir.

Road has been uphill, almost vertical, for years.
A boost to oeconomia most welcome, sir.'

'Say no more. You have my patronage.'
I looked through a large crack in the door

(there *were* many) and saw an old man,
much taller than my small father,

who was so thin, that day his stoop resembling
a frozen bow. The man was much fatter

than Pops too, he was in a word: obesus.
His smooth olive-skinned face wore

the haughty expression of a true patrician,
his thinning brown hair was cut

in the fashionable pudding-bowl haircut,
his orange-and-white-striped toga

was of sumptuous linen that fell in elegant folds,
he wore several gold rings with bright stones

and when my eyes moved slowly down
I saw his legs: thin, hairy *and* bandy.

At which point my own took me rapidly
down the street, not even stopping at Alba's,

no words could form yet.
I ran until I reached the sloping banks

of the River Fleet, far away from the docks,
and then I screamed at the water

until my throat was sore and my spittle
had dried up, not caring

that all the fishermen thereabouts
stopped mending their nets and stared.

I stayed for hours and when it was dark,
the beach deserted, I stripped off, threw

my tatty green dress on to pebbles,
walked into the cold water and swam far out,

shivering. It was what I needed,
to calm me down. I had done it before.

When I turned round, the city was lit up
with lamps, and torches flickered in windows

and doorways of houses on the hills.
I knew I had to accept my fate. I *could* throw

countless tantrums, I *was* an expert,
but it would go ahead, regardless.

The man's voice carried such utter imperium,
and he expressed such an awful desire for me.

I swam towards the lights, forcing myself
to conquer the cold water,

before my body seized up with cramp.
And what about Mater dearest?

Dad would have sent her on an errand.
I thought of how she spat out words

like the gristle of fetid beef, hating
her adopted language, even now:

Zuks! Fetch Khu-kh-umba! Cabb-age!
Hasp-ara-gush!

She'd wave an arm at Dad,
her underarm loose like soggy papyrus.

More! More! – finger and thumb rubbing
together in a greedy money-making gesture.

Nubia good! He'd turn away, serve
another customer, joke with them,

while she scowled, pulled her voluminous
black robes over her head, slumped

into a corner, still as a sack of potatoes.
As a kid, I'd crawl into her covers,

make my breath hers.
A sweet tooth had taken the rest away,

her cheeks were dried out and grooved,
she had given birth when most wombs

nourished ghosts, walked with stillborns
riding her back. She dragged me down streets,

I flew like her robes in fierce wind.
Darling Catullus came three years later,

a miracle on account of his sperm bag.
I hadn't been left to die outside the city walls

exactly, but, aged three, I knew who
would inherit the key to the Kingdom of Pops.

I have suffer so too you will have suffer.
Her eyes were nigrosine, whites browned,

liquefying only when she rocked Catullus
to sleep with softly sung Nubian ditties –

cross-legged on the mat which served
as couch and mattress behind the counter

of our first vegetable shop in Milk Street.
Ulcers sprouted in my mouth, sleepless,

Dad lanced them, I bit my tongue
so's not to awaken the Baby Jesus,

was desperate to run into the night for ever,
to find the river and disappear in it,

I was swimming in the dead of it,
my frozen limbs struggled up the beach,

my dress instantly soaked. I ran back
through the deserted streets,

feeling my blood warm up, my joints
becoming fluid again, the only sound

was of my sandalled feet on hardened earth,
my harsh panting breaths. I called for Alba,

she heard from the back where they slept,
but she came quickly to the door,

took one look at me, ran back inside, returned
to wrap me up in her grey blanket

that scratched my wet skin like thistles.
She made me sit down, just the two of us,

few dared walk around after dark.
She rubbed my back. 'Zeeks. Wassup?'

THE BETROTHAL

His pupils
are soaked in desire,

float in a crisp January sky,
show no mercy,

even as mine plead
innocence.

A small gold link
to my heart

lies in the damp crevice
of his supplicant palm,

spiders crawl
up his forearm,

I am level
with his beige linen

abdomen, black leather girdle,
slung low.

'The Ægyptians,' he proclaims,
'discovered a most delicate nerve

on the finger anularius,
the only one, indeed,

with a direct line
to our greatest gift:

The Human Heart.
And so with this ring, I thee betroth,

Zuleika,
cherished daughter

of our man from Nubia, Anlamani.'
He takes my limp hand,

fills
the trembling gold

and withdraws
ever so,

ever so,
ever so

slowly, to applause, but
I flick my hand down,

so that Cupid's cute
little handiwork

tinkles on the ground,
amidst gasps.

My eyes lock his in
then,

and smile.
He has just made

of my greatest gift
an exile.

OSMOSIS

I

A straw mat, an earth floor,
snow that blew in as we lay, three

in a row, my vigilant Dad shaking
pools of water off the cowhide blanket,

for our poor wooden shop offered
little protection from the storms of winter.

II

He and Mum, way back when,
the family heirloom, he whispered,

was a human chain belonging to the King of Meroe,
with no breakages for generations,

their own mother, his concubine.

Is my mother also my aunt?
Am I your daughter and niece?
Am I my own cousin?

III

Dad looked hurt. They shared
the same profile, I thought tribal.

'There are some things,
you can only share with your own.

When you're a slave you dream
of either owning slaves or freeing them.'

IV

A famine, plague or flood
(the story always changed), the king

died, the palace was in chaos,
they fled 200ks to Khartoum in a caravan,

exporting sacks of sorghum,
lentils and melons.

V

They travelled for a year
before they reached, slept in forests

or inns, sold amethysts and chrisoliths
stolen from the palace, she resisted

every step onwards, yearned
for the city of Meroe, and safety.

VI

They bypassed Rome
and its many Ethiops, too congested

they were told, but they heard
of Londinium, way out in the wild west,

a sea to cross, a man
could make millions of denarii.

VII

I shivered behind his itchy shawl,
he mumbled in his sleep, bristling

with plans, flames burnt
under his clothes, I slid my fingers

into hot armpits, he squeezed, I felt
him draw the ice from my veins.

VIII

Breasts bursting with milk
for the coming Son of Christ

pushed against my back, stealing
my heat, knuckles poked into my spine,

until I melted into sleep and awoke,
not knowing where I began.

TILL DEATH DO US

I

The white stucco villas of Cheapside
are usually out of bounds to scallywags

like me and Alba. Guards shoo us away.
(She has not been invited.) Today

they bow as if I were the emperor's wife,
when my horse-drawn carriage, *if* you please,

arrives at a villa with its very own latrina.
and enough rooms to fill the Forum.

Janus-faced gits! I am the same girl
I was last week. Or am I?

II

A *lady* uses powdered horn to enamel
her teeth, dontcha know, and powdered

mouse brains keep her breath sweet.
I am pampered by maids, an ornatrix is weaving

Indian hair into my own, six pads – Vestal-stylee.
They are painting me white with chalk,

my lips and cheeks with the lees of red wine,
Don't talk! Black ash is dabbed on to my eyes,

Keep still! I'm the It Girl of Londinium, yeah!
Alba would crack up.

III

A girl sits in a silk-embroidered loincloth,
all tarted up with a wedding to go to.

A lemon tunic, a heavy saffron cloak,
a bright yellow veil are all draped over her,

then a wreath of myrtle and orange blossom,
and around her neck, a metal collar. *Here, Fido!*

A lady *never* leaves her cubiculum,
without putting on the slap. Jove forbid,

I should ever again be seen au naturel.
Someone watches me in the mirror.

IV

The haruspex ripped out the guts of a pig,
blood ran down his arm on to the pretty floor.

Ubi tu Felix, ego Zuleika: then Felix *kissed* me.
and the room whirled with dancing girls

exposing their breasts and guests
poured red wine into each other's mouths,

clowns juggled knives and dwarf acrobats
did cartwheels and I entered the statue

of Minerva in the corner, alabaster and wise.
I would soon be alone with him.

V

Felix had to wrest me from Mum's
loving embrace (*what* a performance).

Our cortège turned the midnight streets
into bacchanalia, torches and flutes led the way,

everyone sang bawdy songs and people
danced out of houses, past the baths

and up Cannon Street towards his manor
at the Walbrook Stream. He carried me

over the threshold. I glanced back to see if Alba
was in the crowd, watching.

VI

Flames flickered by the marital bed.
He laid me out, peeled off my layers

like humid rose petals, he sucked my *toes*,
called me *mea delicia*, opened my legs

and held a candle to my vulva until flames
tried to exit my mouth as a scream

but his hand was clamped over it. I passed out.
Pluto came for me that night,

and each time I woke up, it was my first night
in the Kingdom of the Dead.

II

METAMORPHOSIS

Martius: doctor recommends months
of recuperation each time his sewing

is undone, this becomes my world, to adjust
to married life, I am not let out, he says

he is too selfish to share his new bride
just yet, imagine this is our honeymoon,

you are in a cocoon, will emerge
with the manners of a true lady, one day

he will take me to his holiday villa
in the Bay of Neapolis, you have never seen

the like, my dear, stop the tears, my love,
accept your grand new status, I wander

around the villa, grander than any me and Alba
imagined, leading off the atrium

are cubicula, triclinia, bathing rooms
built just for me, the tablinum full of books

where he receives his clients, peristylium
at the back full of bushes and flowers, a kitchen

leads off it, the slaves' quarters hidden
behind trees, by the front door the household

shrine, all this is mine but I am a stranger
here, listen out for him, where is he?

Will he call for me? *Aprilis*: when he leaves,
I fear his return, when he returns, I fear

he will never leave, Mum and Dad visit,
stand like country bumpkins, stare at a twenty-

foot ceiling, speechless, a professor
comes daily, I am reading Juvenal

and his witty works, push my back
into his at night, when he is out I fear

he will never come home, when he is here,
I fear I will be left alone, again,

I am becoming a spectre, I think, *Maius:*
he wakes me up at dawn, three leather trunks

are stacked in the atrium, a chariot
outside will take him across Gaul towards Rome,

he has important duties to perform,
he must report back to HQ, attend

to his business interests. 'The silk route
from China for one, Persian bandits

are plundering my caravans of silk, pirates
are seizing my shipments of grain

from Alexandria, the Med is a war zone,
I must see to all that so we can have all this.

Go out into the town, enjoy, I'll assign
a bodyguard but, for goodness sake,

don't show me up and walk,
take a train of slaves and a sedan.'

TWO HOT CHICKS

'Is it a girl? Is it a ghost? Is it a glamour puss?
Is it a grand dame? No, it's me mate, Zuky-dot!

How've you been, darlin'?' Venus's droll
contralto floated over the empty wooden tables

in her twilight bar Mount Venus, at the junction
of Ludgate Hill and St Paul's Churchyard.

It was late, not quite the done thing for a lady
to be ordering a pint just up from the docks,

in fact to be out alone at all. But Venus and me
went way back to when I was a mite

of seven, scavenging for leftovers at the market
of a Saturday evening in the years

before Dad became a 'man successfully made'.
Venus showed me how to tell the difference

between an overripe apple and a maggoty one,
helped me carry my assortment of cabbages,

turnips, radishes and wotnots home
much to the snooty disdain of Dad,

waiting in the road for supper to arrive,
for Venus was a sight to behold, and some.

'It's a long story,' I called back, all gung-ho,
braving a room acrid with stale beer and vino,

trying to step daintily in my posh new sandals
on a sawdust floor covered with broken glass,

testament to the previous night's round
of ribaldry, rivalry and lewd rhetoric.

We embraced, tears came into my eyes,
partly because she'd just come from the baths

and had overdone it with a mixed potion
of lavender, rose and honeysuckle perfumes

and partly because it had been so long
since I'd been held without it being a precursor

to a demand for sex – non-negotiable.
She fingered my gold dolphin earrings,

her dark blue eyes sparkling with amusement.
'Upmarket tomfoolery, eh. The real thing, luv?'

I had left home that afternoon with wings
on my heels, ordered the sedan-bearers,

bodyguard and train of status symbols
to trot ten paces behind, made a dash for it,

up Bucklersbury and out of sight, headed
for Gracechurch Street, popped in to see Alba,

who was chasing headless chickens in the yard,
before plucking them for display outside.

She couldn't believe it was me.
She moaned she had no time to herself now.

I moaned that was *all* I had. She asked
why I hadn't come out to play,

but I couldn't explain.
I knew she wouldn't understand.

I could tell she was angry. She was catching
chickens, then letting them go.

'Stop and talk to me,' I begged. 'Please.'
'I said it would change, Zee. Look at you,

all poshed up, I went to your house twice
but the guards told me to scarper.'

'It wasn't me,' I replied. 'It's him, it's my . . .
I've missed you so much. It's been awful.'

She stopped running, came over,
awkwardly, not knowing what to do

with her hands, whether to hug me.
'Me too. Look at all that make-up, Zee,

and that dress, you look so grown up.
So when do I get to go to your manor?'

'When I can fix it. Tranio's the head honcho
when he's away, so it won't be easy.'

'I feel sorry for you, Zee.'
'Thanks!'

'No, I'm not being bitchy. I'm just glad
I'm still free. Come and see me soon.'

She disappeared inside the house.
Two doors up, Mater and Pater

were serving a queue of bemused customers.
Dad was chatting his usual bollocks,

about really being the exiled King of Meroe,
the last of the great pharaohs.

'My palace bigger than governor's. Yes. No lie.
I made good, see. Look Zuleika here,

married to Roman nobilitas. Veritas princess?
Clothes so fine? My blood, see.'

Blah, blah, bloody-blah. Mum glared at him,
as usual, whispered loudly he'd taken

to gambling, wanted a villa like Mr Felix.
'Nothing good enough now.

Him want quick-come money.'
She'd found a backgammon board

with rolling dice in the yard, confronted him,
but did he listen to her? She moaned

he spent most evenings in a seedy den
by the river front with a bunch of low-lifes.

I tried to furrow my brow with concern
but felt I was watching a B-rate play

with C-rate actors, sitting in a D-rate seat
at the amphitheatre.

I asked after Little Bro Catullus
(aka *He Who Can Do No Wrong*), was told

he was at Maestro Caesar's over the way.
Took this as my cue to leave, though I just

studied him from a distance while Caesar,
bald as a pumpkin, cut his locks in the middle

of the thoroughfare, waved his knives
at passers-by who got too vocal

with their complaints, had slashed a face
or two in his time, you see.

There the Little Usurper sat, fat brown
cheeks gleaming, full petulant lips,

wearing the smug demeanor of one
so dearly loved he'd been bought a dog,

a parrot *and* a blooming nightingale.
Then Caesar's knife plunged suddenly

into his neck, blood spurted out, Catullus
released a spine-chilling scream, his eyes

rolled back, he fell off his stool
on to the ground, writhing. Yeah, right. I think *not*.

I took to my old stomping ground,
the narrow backstreets, hawkers poked sulphur

matches in my face, or lamps for sale
or bread or second-hand shoes.

'Oh, come on, miss, be a benefactor
to a poor beggar, why don't you?'

'Abi!' I said, telling them I never walked
with cash and that the jewels were fake,

then pushed them roughly aside,
as they had done me, oh not

so many moons ago. A flower-seller
sold vibrant bouquets, an ivory-vendor

sold tusks from Kenya, mirrors hung
from shop doorways, the scent of oils

from Arabia and Ethiopia floated
out of perfumeries, others sold spices

and cotton, there were pearl-sellers,
goldsmiths, robe-makers, cloak-makers,

cabinet-makers, embroiderers, dyers,
tanners, workers sitting on stools outside,

or doors wide open to shops;
money-changers lurked in doorways

like dirty old men, luring me
to make my fortune; I heard horn-tuners,

horses' hoofs, barrels on gravel, chisels
on stone, saws on logs, knives

scraping leather, coppersmiths' tapping,
children's laughter, grunting pigs, sausages

frying in saucepans, chanting schoolboys
sitting under trees, I heard shouts,

bells, gongs, chimes,
how I loved and missed it all.

Outside the Forum, Dinesh the bow-legged
mystic was still doing his old

cobra-in-a-basket act with a reed whistle,
though the viper was geriatric,

could no longer writhe its alluring,
double-jointed body in a dance

that would feed Dinesh's family daily.
He stood alongside the local loonies

on wooden crates who predicted
the destruction of empire or that Christianity

would soon come west, cracking jokes
about virgins giving birth or how

to walk on water without getting your feet wet
or the ten best ways to rise from the dead

or declaring Jupiter is really a woman
or that raw eggs give you a longer hard-on

or parading in a papyrus placard announcing
that the world will end in the year 300 –

to a crowd of onlookers who kept up a steady
supply of rotten fish and pigs' entrails.

Inside the orators were out in full force, juicing
every syllable for its music, competing

to speak the most passionalissima Latin
to a lively audience. I slid in at the back,

desperate to know about the world I lived in.
They spoke of the great Septimius Severus,

who had gone from African boy
to Roman emperor, had spent many years

travelling the empire from Germania
to Syria, back to his hometown in Libya,

who would surely one day visit Britannia,
this far-flung northern outpost of empire,

defeat the fucking Scots, Pict and Saxon
bastards who made a steady onslaught

on our cities and towns, spear every last man
of them, burn their villages, castrate

their infant sons, occupy their women,
colonize their terra firma, make them speak

our lingo, impose taxes, yay! and thus
bring Pax Romana to this our blessed island.

Vivat Emperor Sevva!
Vivat Emperor Sevva!

* * *

'The first time is always the worst, Zuky-doo.'
Venus had listened to each scene in my drama

Girl Weds Rich Old Man Who Locks Her Up.
'I know, believe you me, I couldn't sit for days.'

She crossed her eyes, sucked in her cheeks,
affected a shrug and we burst out laughing,

though mine came with a few tears, unwittingly.
I saw Venus afresh, noticed that under the slap

her features were drawn, her bright-red
lips were miserable when immobile.

'Wassup?' I ventured quietly.
Her staff were drifting in, sweeping the floor,

fetching water, lighting lanterns.
Outside the street was coated with black.

'Nuffink to speak of.'
Her face suddenly crumpled into her right hand.

'Show must go on an' all that.'
'No, really, tell me,' I insisted, realizing

for the first time that Venus was my alma mater,
but that I knew Sweet FA about the desires

beneath the glamorous alter ego of glitz and wit,
had never really cared before.

I sat up, astonished at the revelation
that this was probably My First Adult Thought.

She looked me straight in the eyes,
not one ounce of glitter. 'It's like this.'

She slumped forward on the table,
both hands now cradling her face, pushing

her chalky white flesh into high cheekbones.
'You're either a figure for fucking or a fucking freak.

Everyone needs a one-and-only after a while.
I'm twenty-two, Zuky-do. Middle aged!

A Venus must 'ave an Adonis.
Even if it's just for a while. Bronzed, rippling,

adoring, preferably, compliant, essentially.
Someone to come home to, to cook

a pease pudding for of a winter's night.
Look at the facts.

Thousands of bloody years ago
the Ægyptians believed in a sparring partner,

a Mr and Mrs scenario, I'll stand by you,
mi' amore, if you stand by me.

Why can't I have it too? I'll never have children.
No Cupid to match-make us mere humans.

You and Alba are my sprogs,
but I need a husband! Not a touch-your-toes-

and-it'll-be-ten-bucks-more number.
Flippen 'eck! I need a bona fide husband!

I need a C-O-N-I-U-N-X!
Whadoesthatspell? Husband!'

She jumped up from her seat, began shouting
at her staff, 'Get a move on, you bunch

of loafers, no-hopers, trollops and has-beens.
The punters'll be here soon. Get your glad rags,

falsies and wigs on. You look a state!
I'm going out for a bit and if this taverna

ain't spick and span by the time
I get back, you'll be joining the paupers

queuing for handouts outside the mansions
of Cheapside on the morrow!'

She turned back to me.
'Let me ball-of-chalk you home, darlin'.

You're a woman of means now.
Ain't no scamp no more.

Prime target for muggers and ne'er-do-wells.'
'Yeah, right,' I replied. 'What does Juvenal say?

Never go out to supper without
having first made your will.'

'My dee-yah! You'll be quoting Plato next!'
'Actually, I've been studying poetry

with my professor, Theodorous.
I'm going to become a great poet.

I'd love to be famous for something.
Felix wants me educated, so how can he object?'

I pulled my brown woollen shawl over my head,
'Good,' she said, putting an arm around me.

'Keep you out of trouble.
Just make sure you write witty ditties about me.

I wanna be immortalized, dontchaknowit,
and ain't no one never gonna write

about your life but you. Once you're dead,
you never existed, baby, so get to it.'

Two heads taller than me, she steered me past
the brothel at the corner, its owner a man

from Gaul with a wet donkey's tail
of a moustache, who used to call out:

'I 'ave a Woppy, a Chinky, a Honky, a Paki,
a Gingery, an Araby, now all I need is a Blackie.

'Ow's about it, leetle girlie?'
In the old days Venus slapped his face

if he propositioned me, though
tonight his jaw dropped when I passed by,

transformed into a real uptown chick, I was.
Venus and I chuckled as we navigated

the dockland streets, slipping
on the slimy contents of chamber pots

thrown from the tenements.
She had long been a fantastic sight

in our town, originally from Camulodunum
on the east coast, she had acquired

an affected mockney accent,
part of *me re-invention package, my dee-yah!*

Fair hair was dyed black, piled with curly
hairpieces, wooden pattens raised

her sandals an unheard-of three inches
off the ground, and her feet were as large

as any man's. In her off-the-shoulder gowns
and dolled-up face, hair showed

where breasts usually sprouted. She used
to be followed by hordes, pelted with stones,

but folks got used to her,
most didn't give a damn and those who

did found their faces re-structured,
for it was not wise to bring out the man

in Venus, née Rufus.
Mount Venus was a haven for her kind,

men who loaned themselves out for cabarets
or private parties for rich married men

who liked the best of both sexes, disappeared
into the back room for anonymous antics.

Others just liked to parade in chic gowns.
The sassiest called out to soldiers from the bar,

'Ditch the beard for the lipstick, bay-bee!
and life'll *never* be the same again!'

to hoots of laughter. Alba and me were their pets,
allowed to watch and giggle, promising

not to tell a soul when a famous lawyer
or butch centurion emerged

from the back room unsteady on his legs,
in a wig, torn gown and smudged lipstick.

The first time we met, me and Alba
had joined in with a crowd throwing stones

at her as she sashayed up Newgate Street,
cream veil swept over her shoulder,

and a shopping basket swinging at her side.
She chased and easily caught us,

and was about to land us one
when she clocked we were 'stinkin' little raggas'

and released us with an earful of expletives.
Fascinated, we followed her every time

we saw her after that, stood outside her club
until she invited us in on condition

we sat quietly in the corner.
She once confided to us that at our age

she loved to rub the soft fabrics
of her sister's dresses against her cheeks

and prance around in them to much laughter
from her parents; but many years later,

when they discovered her doing the same
and sneaking out to date a local shepherd boy

at night, they kicked her out.
She'd not seen them since, and felt brutally

severed from her past, blanking
it all out to survive.

She came to Londinium, aged fourteen,
feeling like an orphan who quickly

became an urchin, a rent boy in fact, working
in the shadows of Spitalfields Cemetery after hours.

But she'd inherited her father's ambition
and business acumen. The result?

Spank (saucy panties and nookie kit),
a shop for the lady with a prick and no tits,

but the clientele was pathetically small,
so after much market research Mount Venus

was created to fill the gap in the club market,
and was making a pile.

'The thing is,' she'd say, 'a life without a past
is a life without roots. As there's no one

holding on to me ankles I can fly anywhere,
I became the woman you see before you.'

We didn't understand much of it then,
but whatever Venus said was memorabile

and over the years her words sailed
back into mind and made sense.

* * *

I was glad of the escort home.
Felt vulnerable, never had before,

when I was nil, when I was *one of us*.
Tranio was waiting at the porticus for me,

a veritable Vesuvius eruptus bursting
in his neat little grey tunic, black hair

coming out of nostrils, ears, neck
and so thick on his legs no skin showed.

A torch was shaking in his hairy hand.
He opened his gob: 'The master ordered me

to keep an eye on you, missy ma'am.
It is my duty to inform you –'

I swept past him, I was the *madam*, after all.
He was my *slave*, after all.

Venus rolled her eyes at me, I whispered
she'd get an invite to a private do chez moi

next time Felix exited-off on
one of his long-distance gallivants,

and I'd tested the boundaries
enough to do what I liked when he was gone.

I blew a kiss from the doorway, watched
her hobble back into the night, raising her skirts

over the open drains, exposing
discus-thrower's calves (thankfully waxed).

I would have more days out on the town.

SISTERFAMILIAS
(Relative Values)

A girl certainly knows
where she stands when a Grand Matron

of Rome-cum-Orgy Queen
comes a-visiting this *quaint little town*

or *dump,* depending on her alcohol
intake or stage of premenstrual tension.

The Divine Antistia
was Felix's younger sister, twice married,

twice widowed, stinking rich
and top of the A list of every feast

between the Palatine Hill
and palazzi of Neapolis.

Days before the dominatrix
was borne in on a gilded sedan,

PAs arrived, cooks were installed
in the kitchen, invites sent to VIPs,

and the guest room decked out
with chains, whips and a life-size crucifix.

'So! This is *Illa Bella Negreeta!*'
she purred, billowing towards me

in dazzling turquoise silks,
bright gemstones on every finger,

a face fashionably white with lead
and pouting ochre-red lips.

'Cute, yes. Young, even better.
Stupid, no doubt.' Her violet eyes

ran slowly over my flesh
and singed every invisible hair.

She brushed lightly past,
talking loudly down the hallway.

'Come, Felix, a hog on a spit
and flagons of wine await us,

though I'd prefer little wifey here,
hottie, plumpie and my sweet juices

dripping on to her wagging tongue.
You *lucky* boy.'

What Antistia wanted
Antistia got, but I was Felix's missus

and protected. She stayed
two weeks. Felix came to bed at dawn,

if at all, insisted I bolt the door
until he knocked.

I heard clowns, poets, castanets
and much guffawing in the atrium,

followed by screams deeper
into the night, which held no real pain,

strangely, and sometimes a child's,
which did.

'You will never be one of us.'
At fourteen I was no longer a novelty.

After eight courses, Antistia swooned,
her Medusa-style wig fell over her eyes,

a coma loomed if she did not finger
her throat to start again.

'A real Roman is born and bred,
I don't care what anyone says,

and that goes for the emperor too,
jumped-up *Leeebyan*. Felix will never

take you to Rome, Little Miss *Nooobia*,
he has his career to think of.'

My tongue became wood.
I could never speak in her presence

or to Felix's cronies, who spoke
as if they owned the world. Well,

I guess they did. My words revealed me,
their ornate diction was a mask.

Felix's father had been a governor,
they had dined with the emperor's children,

my father spoke pidgin-Latin,
we ate off our laps in the doorway,

splattered with mud. Yet I was Roman too.
Civis Romana sum. It was all I had.

ZULEIKA AND HER GIRLS

Two ginger girls arrived, captured
up north, the freckled sort (typical

of Caledonians). Felix ordered them
before he left for Rome.

When approached, they clawed the air
with filthy talons, mucus ran in clotted rivers

from pinched little noses,
their eyes were splattered mosquitoes,

courtesy of Tranio, to shut them up.
Fascinating, so vile, yet something

just for me, id and ego. Pets.
I ordered Tranio to chain them

to the jasmine tree and went to bed.
But savages were in my peristylium,

sweet jasmine became the foulest dung,
I heard the pad of feet, my door flew open,

vulgar babble, quickly overcome,
my limbs were torn off like rabbit legs,

scalped, my brains scooped out
like lumps of congealed maggots,

dribbling from lascivious mouths,
my sex carved out, stuck on a spear

as a bloody trophy, before they escaped
out the window and climbed

on to the roof, howling. I awoke.
Cold to the marrow. Alone.

Tranio! Shut those fucking cats up!
First light, to Huggin Hill Baths

on a chain. Tranio flung them
into the hot water of the caldarium

(*such* a tantrum), then on to a marble slab;
oil and pumice was rubbed

into their ribby little bodies and rolls of dirt
scraped off with a strigil.

I was eating a sausage and I must say,
it almost made me nauseous.

Next, my hairdresser, dressmaker,
manicurist, until, as they are now,

little ladies: their red curls piled high
are charmed serpents, and white lead

thankfully subdues their flecking.
Valeria and Aemilia, I call them,

and I hope they will become –
my devotees.

ANOTHER WORLD, NATALE SOLUM
(Native Soil)

Extracting stones from dates,
a delicate task, to leave the flesh intact,

a rare treat to be allowed inside the culina –
only when Felix and Tranio were out

and Cook had gone to the market.
I could pretend – my very own kitchen:

brazier in a corner, hare strung up
by its legs, amphorae against the wall,

baskets of vegetables, bunches of herbs,
beef stew simmering, table in the middle,

us three around it. Aemilia –
her chest like a washboard, a timorous voice,

when she spoke, which was hardly ever.
I still struggled with their strange pidgin.

At my side, Valeria, of late the Voluptuaria,
always the more loquacious of the two.

This afternoon she was on a roll.
'Mammy an Faither were chieftens, ye ken.'

(Oh, really, where had I heard *that* before.)
'Oor hame was a big roon stone hoose.

De hail of oor village could feast inower it.
After wark, everyone gaithered for denner,

we'd sit cross-legged in a big raing,
an eat breid an stew out of wuiden bowlies.

Efterwards de Druids would tell stories
aboot de goads, oor granfaither

was chief Druid, he could confabble wi thaim.'
'Put the stones in the bin, Aemilia.

Now let's fill them with the pine kernels,
and a dash of pepper.'

Our hands worked slowly. Time was ours.
'Ye had to gae through a guarded gate

fir we were ayeways being attacked by tribus.
Mammy would leid de sodgers into battle,

hir lang heir flying behind like fire,
standing on hir chariot she was so ferox,

all in de scud, face pentit blue wi an owl
tattooed on it, horse on hir stomach,

lowping salmon on hir feet.
She's always thraw de firsten javelin,

then skedaddled, yellyhooin like daft.
We'd watch from de safety of de hill-heid.'

'Here's the salt.' I sprinkled some from a pot
on to a plate. 'Roll the dates in it.'

I went over to the hot brazier,
poured honey into a pan. 'Bring them over.'

What was this fantastic tale she told?
Was the world outside such a strange place?

'Is this story for real?' I challenged.
'Whit dae ye mean?' she shot back.

I let it go, tossed dates into sizzling honey,
a matter of minutes and they would

be succulent temptresses, ready
for his highness's dessert at dinner.

'How did you end up at York?'
'One tid we were attacked in de nicht,

no one expecked it wi de sey so roch,
Mam was killed ootricht,

hir heid taeken away on a spear.
Us girls an Faither were taeken as sclaves

down to York an when we got there
he was taeken by an agent to Gaul.

We were sold at auction an de rist,
as ye ken, is historia.'

'Yes, and you arrived like wailing beasts.'
'We were so afeared when we saw ye.

We'd niver seen a bleck afore.
Terrible things had happened to us.'

So, this was all about sympathy.
But how could I put balm on their wounds

when my own were still so raw?
Suffering? Join the club, girls.

'Madam, worse was to come . . . Tranio . . .'
'Enough!' I cut her off, surprising myself,

but this little bonding exercise had to stop.
Anger had surged up from my depths

before I could recognize it.
'You will have your manumission when I die.'

Where did that come from?
Their heads fell. Silence.

So this was really a bid for liberty.
'There's no way Felix will free you now.'

I heard a sniffle from Aemilia.
I wanted to order her to stop,

after all, my well was full, was it not?
I carefully spooned the glittering,

honey-soaked dates out of the pan.
'Aemilia, put them on a silver plate,

we three will eat them in the peristylium,
until all the sweetness is inside us.'

III

PRIMUM DETERGE EAM
(Wipe It First)

A mural on three walls: cloudy blue skies,
a pale green lake with water lilies,

a brown swan; water-nymphs bathe
under a weeping willow, sloping shoulders,

generous hips, chunky beige thighs
with cellulite, calves taper to ankles thin

as thumbs. Carved into the wooden door
a Cupid with thick curls, his arrow aims

straight at me. The floor has shocking-pink
love hearts inside yellow square tiles;

a glass window opens on to the peristylium.
The Mistress of the House

is left to muse alone each morning,
because the Master of the House installed

only one swirling-pink marble seat
with gold trimmings in this, his magnificum

Templum of Excrementum.
I feel the snakes breathe of the early sun,

sweat streaks down my arms
as I struggle to release yesterday's gourmet

cuisine, processed, mashed-up, trying
to burst forth into the aqueduct below.

I recall the camaraderie of the public latrinae.
Two dolphins leapt over the entrance,

the world of grown-ups: who was shagging
whom, the price of beef, which official

took bribes, the best way to make
your own beer. The concerted family effort –

Dad on one side, Mops on t'other,
me and Catoo in the middle, little brown

batties frozen numb in winter, sponge sticks
in buckets of water at the ready;

the crumbling, one-armed statue
of the Goddess Fortune presiding over

a semicircle of twelve ardent excreters,
her noseless smile blessing us

with health and happiness.
Dad's instructions:

'One, two, tree and puuuussssh!'
And we did, regular as the water clock Felix

bought for the atrium as soon
as they became the latest *must have, darling*

of every upper-class domus Londinii.
How many years ago? I had lost count.

I am done.
Nostalgia is a most efficient enema.

I walk into the atrium, gaze up
at the square hole of sky. You see, our villa

is built in the fashionable style of the Med,
as Felix always boasts.

'Great for British winters,' I once replied,
as snow fell on to the frozen fountain,

its centrepiece a statue of a snarling Medusa
(a strange choice, but Felix believed

low-class intruders would fear
they'd be turned to stone, and backtrack).

Water poured out of her open mouth,
and her flying dreadlocks, which normally

produced fine sprays,
had grown icicle extensions.

I snapped one off and sucked.
Felix's face froze too, then a flame

of irritation swept up from lips to forehead,
not igniting into rage as expected

but metamorphosing strangely into desire.
A difficult one this, not wanting to arouse either.

He has grown more fond of me than expected.
He needs me to love him, methinks.

He wants to reach out to me,
but he can't reveal himself –

the son of a patrician is not taught how.
Sometimes he curls his arms around me

at night as if I am the most precious
thing in his world, as if I am his soul

and without me he would be empty.
You make life real, he'd often said.

Instead of a list of goals achieved.
That was as far as he could take it.

I search his grey eyes, notice the blue
film of old age beginning to show,

their whites are the colour of yolk; bones
which pushed out pale brown cheeks

are buried, puffy skin swings in pouches
from a jaw where it had stuck to it,

I imagine. He was young once, I think.
Husband, I know you not. Do I want to?

A smirk whispers on my lips,
but before he is sure it exists I flash

my cutesy *Little Miss Innocens Smile* –
he is a sucker for it.

'But of course we have central heating,'
I add.

CAPISTRUM MARITALE

(The Matrimonial Halter)

– JUVENAL

I

Ripples in your watery skin,
unseen beneath the volume

of groans. I hover
above the marital bed, the cat-gut

seams of our mattress split.
(3 courses, not 8, should suffice, mea delicia.)

II

Legs straight, you like me tight,
it is your size (and shame),

you tore me unformed,
drew blood before eggs ripened.

If I had a little girl . . .
I would call her . . . Claudia.

III

I have known only this, a shiver,
a million dreams expelled:

'Was I good?' *Magnifico!* I gasp,
floating down, swim

to the wash bowl, your dead sons
trickling down my legs.

MODUS VIVENDI
(A Way of Living)

'Good morning, madam.'
Ah! Tranio, Felix's bulldog, who lurks

behind columns as if spying in an ancient drama
on a demonic wife about to be caught

at adultery or infanticide or fratricide
or matricide or patricide.

He is short, less than five foot, and bulky,
walks as if bearing a sack of cabbages,

supervises the other subordinates
(I think we have fifty) with a gruff

street-seller's voice which reverberates
around the villa the entire day,

even when one is trying to siesta.
The legion of mice emerges noisily at dawn,

in plain regulation black tunicas and sandals.
They scurry up ladders to sponge

down pillars, wipe the gilded bronze statues
of the gods, clean oil lamps, draw water

from our well, empty the charcoal braziers,
dust the altar, weed the peristylium,

do the laundry. I sometimes think
that if we had fewer of them there'd be less

cleaning to do, is it not their dead skin
that creates most of the dust?

'How is madam today?'
He regards me with a subtle loathing,

I always feel it in my stomach, it does not
surface on to his face – so still

you sense he is a man of troubled passions.
I used to think the primary one was hate,

but today I am convinced the deeper one
is despair. His brows are stitched into a bushy

black line which splits his face into two parts.
It has always irked me. He *needs* a wife,

to set a pair of tweezers on them.
Tranio entered Blighty as Felix's manservant,

a ruthless sycophant, promotion
to Head Honcho was swift.

He surely takes the girls as he pleases,
a perk, but, as I stare him out

in this suspended moment, the clamour
of housework a faraway din, I realize

I have never seen him smile or joke.
He will die with no laughter lines.

'I'm as well as can be expected,' I reply softly,
conscious that my voice carries

a new awareness. I meant to say I was fine
in my usual dismissive manner

that barely conceals the sentiment:
As if *you* care.

'And how are you . . . Tranio?'
I ask, for the first time, ever.

I am supposed to run this household,
but he took all responsibility away

when I was newly-wed. I was a child,
sensed his resentment at my arrival,

at the attention I got from the master,
and he wanted a piece of me too,

the only woman in the house unattainable.
I would feel his hot breath on my neck

when I had not heard his footsteps precede it.
Would run and hide under a couch.

'As well as can be expected, madam.'
We do not look away.

'Yes,' I say. 'You need a wife,'
then rush past him before I see his eyes

spring out of their sockets and bounce
up and down on spongy tendons.

I add, 'I will persuade Felix,'
and I am off, with nothing to do,

but hot coals under my soles.

DOESN'T TIME FLY WHEN YOU'RE HAVING FUN

My brain is dripping
through to the floor, my light

blue robe is the sky
and the sky seeps

into my skin, clings
to my damp bloated breasts, gathers

in a pool
at the top of my sodden thighs;

the appalling sweetness of honeysuckle
suffocates

my breathing, my ribcage
is crushing my lungs. I am dizzy.

I am cloying,
my flesh has sunk

into the lumpy straw stuffing
of my chaise longue,

my bones are welded to the frame,
I will melt into a pool

on the ground,
I will vaporize, a puff of steam,

and my lengthy epitaphium,
listing my great achievements:

Zuleika Woz 'Ere.

Valeria and Aemilia do not work
hard enough, the peacock fans I bought

last week barely flutter either side of me.
They complain of tiredness.

'Madam, oor arms ache so.'
I take a deep breath, though it will wear

me out, and tell them that dragging
boulders of granite in a convoy

of this nation's bipedal exports across
the midday deserts of Ægypt will help enrich

their understanding of the word *tired*.
At last the muted pad of a gong sounds,

my bath is ready, Cornelia my masseuse
awaits me, her fingers possess

the delicate touch of a flautist coupled
with the strength of an ironmonger.

If I am good to Felix, she comes every day,
if not, I do without. (*Such*

is the price of a blow job.)
The price of wealth is solitary bathing.

Valeria and Aemilia wait at the side,
legs dangling over high stools, calves

criss-crossed with thin leather straps.
I wish we could talk as girlfriends

but for some reason all they ever do
is agree with me. Spineless creatures!

My splashes echo around the walls
of this hollow room, pastel paintings

of scantily clad maidens by the lake
at Parnassus (my husband *is* obsessed).

I plunge down, hold my breath, ponder
the merits of never surfacing. Who will miss me?

After I have been oiled and scraped,
with all the finesse of a chef priming a skinned

pig for marinating, after I have been rubbed
and squeezed with all the finesse

of an expert baker and my body sizzles
like frying bacon, the girls dress me.

Later, Mops and Pops will dine with me.
When the patronus is at home

we have more salubrious visitors, such as

whoever he wants a favour from
whoever he wants to do business with
whoever he owes a favour to
whoever he has to bribe
whoever is a relative *and* well connected
whoever is handing out OREs that year.

Anyone not fulfilling the above criteria
don't get no invite. (Jove forbid

any of my pals should find themselves
sandwiched between a senator

and the governor in a reclining threesome
on a couch at a slap-up Chez Felix

when he is in residence.
Come to think of it, Venus would love it.

Alba too.) The wives of the Great and Good
talk over my shoulder – Antistia was spot on,

I will never be a Grand Dame
with a face of stale dough, cracks and all.

I am so used to eating alone, in company.
But a dusky maiden knows,

through their terrified glacier smiles
and the hungry eyes of their husbands

who will strip her naked and fling her
on the floor in the blinking nanosecond

of a Rapid Eye Movement,
that she is a knock-out objet d'art;

though it was a touch
disconcerting years ago, when she was eleven.

AB ASINO IANAM
(Wool from an Ass)

The Gracechurch Mob were late as usual.
I had been pacing the triclinium:

twenty-four strides in length, fourteen in width,
the mosaic pebble floor consisted

of six large concentric circles in a row,
grey on blue. The walls depicted

The Rape of Persephone in four gory stages –
all flailing limbs, flowing locks, a torn frock,

red streaks, screaming handmaidens,
a bearded Pluto, thunderous greys,

a pitchfork, wing'd babies. (Quite.)
An inscription on a wall read:

I Do not cast lustful glances at another man's wife.
II Do not be coarse in your conversation.
III Restrain from getting angry.
IV If you cannot abide by these rules, go home.

I wondered if my husband had thought
of telling his guests how to breathe, perhaps?

'Now, now, my good man, lead way.'
They had arrived. Dad was always pompous

with Tranio, hiding a multitude of nouveau riche
insecurities. It was another matter

with his son-in-law, grovelling so much
he might as well have walked

behind him on all fours, head nodding
like a mechanical wooden dog.

Under Felix's patronage, Dad's business
had expanded: he now owned six shops

spread throughout the city, had a staff
of fifteen, spent his days on inspection tours;

his gambling was also thankfully under control.
The door opened. Tranio entered.

'Madam, your father Anlamani, your mother
Qalhata, your brother Catullus.'

'Gratias, Tranio.' We had not met since morning.
We smiled at each other, for the first time,

ever. Mine swelled with gratitude
that perhaps we could be friends?

And only then did I realize that the sack
of cabbages had really been on my back,

he was not hunched at all, it was *I* who felt lighter.
He did need some dental care, I noticed,

when he smiled. I would see to an extraction.
Dad swaggered in as if he were the master

returning home and I the lowly visitor. Typical
behaviour when Felix was in absentia,

his swishy-swashy blue silk toga
over his swishy-swashy green silk tunica,

much too hip for a man his age, his wrinkled
brown left hand bearing gold rings studded

with huge ruby, garnet and plasma stones.
Mum slouched behind him in her black garb

as usual, head to toe, showing only hands
and face. She eyed the triclinium

as if she'd never seen it before, squinting
as if it were some dirty ghetto hovel.

My brother trailed behind in layers of trendy
yellows and oranges which illuminated

his gleaming blue-black skin like a torch.
He too had benefited from my husband's patronage,

the subsequent improvement in family diet –
had grown two heads taller than all of us,

yet still he possessed the soft, squidgy-lipped
face of the little boy I'd kick in the shins

when no one was looking.
We took our seats, Dad on the central couch,

Catullus on the right, me on the left, Mum
squatting on the floor in front of the table,

right in the path of the servers.
(You really couldn't take her anywhere.)

I bit into a sausage, scooped up a couple
of oysters, some salad, drank hot spiced wine

guaranteed to numb an agitated soul.
It was by official decree that only my family

could be trusted to dine with me
when His Highness was away. I dreamt

of the day I could hold my own parties.
Years ago I'd order in a singer, puppeteer or acrobat,

but I was a descendant of philistines,
who ignored them. Nuff said.

Today I derived my entertainment
from watching Little Bro eat,

quite fascinating, filling up his plate
in a panic if it were only three quarters full.

No self-control, you see, will eat
until he explodes, for his hunger is bottomless,

the result of having a great floppy tit
stuffed into his mouth whenever he cried,

yay! right up to the age of seven.
I have spent years pondering this lot,

it keeps the mind a-whirring.
'So! So! So!' Dad sang out. He slurped

an oyster from its shell, looked so awkward
eating lying down, never did back at Chez His.

'So! So! So!' he repeated, almost bald now,
his head a shiny walnut, tufts

of off-white cotton wool poking out
over his ears, his eyelids drooping with age,

two mud pools, heavy and impenetrable,
lurking underneath the hoods.

'I have importans news. Catullus is on up and up.'
He bit into a chicken leg, picked its threads

out of his teeth, made a sucking sound
with his tongue and lips, continued,

'My boy Catullus, my boy . . .'
'I know he's your son, Dad.'

'Don't be so impudens, girlie. I still your pater.
Show respect.'

Yeah, yeah, yeah, I thought, the father
who sold his daughter to the highest bidder.

Don't think I've forgotten or forgiven, buster.
'Tain't in my nature. I smiled affectionately.

'I know that too, Pops.'
We had never had a proper conversation,

whatever I said or however I said it
was always adjudged a big diss.

Sometimes I craved for the olden times
when he meant the world to me

(a time when my brain wasn't fully developed).
He waved an arm to his right,

'Catullus, sonny. Speak!'
But the Son of Sons was lost

in the Kingdom of Food, only a thump
on his back

while he sucked on a chicken leg
dangerously near his oesophagus

would jolt him out of it.
I snickered to myself, looked over at Mum,

but she'd stopped eating,
was thin as a liquorice stick, preferred

maize and bean stew to haute cuisine any day.
'So who's rude, Dad?' I nodded at the gannet.

'You too rude.' He looked askance at me,
stood up, adjusted his robes

at the shoulders, cleared his throat.
'This boy, this good Romanissimus boy,

of Nubian ancestors, whose parents sailed
single-handedly up Great River Nile;

this Catullus, my filius; Grandson of my Father;
Great Grandson of my Father's Father;

Father of my Future Grandchild; Grandfather
of my future Great Grandson; Uncle

to *your* Children (*ahem!*); Great Uncle
to their Children; Beloved Son of his Beloved

Mother, her Mother (his Grandmother)
and her Mother's Mother (his Great Grandmother).

So! This predecessor of those to come after;
this future ancestor and yet today, here

and now, last in line of all ancestors
going back to time beginning;

this ingeniosus boy has been accepta
at top public school for patricians in Roma.

Yes, to train to be officer in triumphant military.
I so proud.' Tears filled his eyes.

I looked around at the cheering millions.
'Fab!' I said, feeling the contents

of my meal churn in my stomach
like straw being mixed to make brick.

Such is the power of nepotism, my brother
the demi-god can barely string a sentence

together for all his educatio.
'Congratulations, brother dearest.

When are you going?'
He looked up absent-mindedly, blood

had been diverted on a desperate mission
from his brain to his intestines

to work his digestive juices.
'Eh? Eh? You thaid thomething?'

His balls had not yet dropped, he was still
the lisping pipsqueaker of yore. *Shame.*

'Congratulations,' I repeated.
'Oh, that,' and he went back to his True Love.

'How soon do thee depart?'
'Eh? Eh?' He looked up again. 'Oh . . . er, thoon.'

'Good,' I muttered, then said aloud,
'Good for you.'

I glanced over at the Virgin Mary.
She just sat there, her robes about her

like a black puddle, gazing at her one and only,
tears streaming down her cheeks.

'My boy,' she said softly, wiping her nose
with her right sleeve from cuff to shoulder.

'What a wonderful world we live in,'
I said aloud to no one in particular

and no one in particular was listening.
Dammit! Words were forming like rusty nails

in my mouth, coating my tongue,
scraping my gums. I spat them out at Dad:

'I've been writing poetry!'
But he'd over exerted himself, poor love,

his head propped up on one arm,
was nodding off.

'Poetry?' he replied eventually, an eye opening.
'Yes! I've been studying it with my professor,

Theodorous, in my Greek Lit. in Translation class.
He said it was absolutely imperative

that I speak Ancient Greek, but I said learning
one alphabet in a lifetime was enough, actually.

He made me read Homer's *Iliad*,
which I found bloody tedious, quite frankly.

All about the siege of Troy. I mean, who cares?
Just an intsy-wintsy bit old-fashioned?

Theodorous says I shouldn't write poetry
until I've studied the last thousand years

of the canon, learnt it off by heart
and can quote from it at random, *and* imitate it

before attempting my own stuff, and he says
it's imperative I start with hendecasyllables

à la Pliny Jr, but I retaliated, saying
I found the lot of it B-O-R-I-N-G,

to be honest, and then he really lost it,
said poetry's supposed to be difficult 'cos

it's high art, otherwise any Tom, Dick
or Hortensius would understand it, yeah!

Then he made me learn Virgil's *Aeneid*
off by heart for my Roman History class.

It's all about the founding of Rome. And it's,
oh, only twelve books long. Contemporary

'cos it's oh, only over two hundred years old.
You should hear him go on about Virgil,

noster maximus poeta, about how
the *Aeneid* will still be a classic text

in two millennia from now. As *if*.
Says all the notable poets were men, except

for some butch dyke who lived with a bunch
of lipstick lesbias on an island in Greece,

but she was really a minor poet and did
I know what asclepiad meant? Or trochee?

Or spondee? Or dactyl? Or cretic? No?
Oh, surprise, surprise! Well, when I did, then

I could give him backchat, and anyway
I'd never write good poetry because what did

I know about war, death, the gods
and the founding of countries?

But you see, Dad, what I really want to read
and hear is stuff about us, about now,

about Nubians in Londinium, about men
who dress up as women, about extramarital

peccadilloes, about girls getting married
to older men and on that note,

in the words of the great god Pliny,
the one too early and the other too late (ahem!).

And I don't care about the past
and I ain't writing for posterity –

he also says I should write for readers
five centuries hence.

Well, I'm a thoroughly modern miss
and who knows what life will be like then,

the Caledonians could rule the world for all we know.
So! So! So! I've started composing a few ditties.

At last I've found a way to express myself.
I know they're not brilliant yet, but you see,

if I keep at it . . . Watch . . . this . . . space!
Do you want to hear one?'

I was exhausted, my cheeks burnt,
my fists were clenched, my chest was tight,

I was frowning, I was frothing, I *would*
make contact with the aliens.

He-ll-oo-oo? Anyone ho-oo-me?
He was silent for a while, then just when

I thought he'd nodded off, he looked up,
made a sweeping pregnant-belly gesture.

'Tu,' he said, in a throaty, sleepy voice.
'What?' I replied.

'When you go make bambino?'
Oh, sod off, you fucking wanker!

nearly tumbled out of my mouth.
'Make soon, be a bona girl for your pater.'

Oblivious, Mum got up to leave, shook
the crumbs from her gown, went to sit

cross-legged on the portico, gazed
longingly at a star-filled night.

I ordered the servers to clear the table,
at which point Catullus's hearing

immediately improved and he quickly piled
as much as possible on to his plate,

and went into mastication overdrive, veins
popping up on his perspiring temples.

They left, eventually. The bloated
and boozed-out Boy Wonder was helped

into the carriage by three nightwatchmen.
The black ate them up. I looked up at the sky

Mum had been studying.
It was not one and the same.

IV

IMPORTANT MATTERS OF STATE

A girl's gotten used to having six legs
instead of the common-or-garden two,

after all, one don't want one's glorious stola
trailing in the dirt no more, innit. Especially

when it's an orange and green damask
check with twisted gold thread, designed

by her favourite couturier Emporio Valentino.
My sedan awaits me and a train

of six slavelings – young boys, chosen
for their uniform height, curly hair

and handsome, big-nosed looks.
The sedan is custom-made,

pig-and cow carvings adorn its wooden sides,
its maker's little joke no doubt.

Felix astonishes me, so lofty, yet no eye
for a workman's act of subversion.

My four bronzed sedan-bearers are waiting,
ex-charioteers fallen on hard times,

uniquely in this household, employees,
their bulging arms could crush a girl like me

(I do imagine it from time to time).
I get in, draw back the muslin drapes,

the sun is slithering down into the faraway
ocean, the air is beginning to tang,

my dear Alba awaits me.
I am borne into town where the workers

are on go-slow, we are not used
to these freak heat waves, but insipid

grey skies ten months of the year,
and insipid blue ones for two.

I take the path of the Walbrook Stream.
Alba's husband owns a small whitewashed villa

at Great Swan Alley, part of a new
development for the middle-class,

middle-income bracket.
Faeces float on the water,

I doubt you can drink from it these days,
and the verge is packed with the poor

out fishing, children skinny-dipping, the path
is clogged up with traffic, although bumpy,

it is more scenic than the road.
We reach the footbridge, turn left up

Copthall Avenue and we are almost there.
Alba's house has six rooms – she too married well,

but, whereas she stopped at four rungs,
I went straight to the top.

She is waiting in the doorway, calling out
to neighbours. Spotting my entourage

a long way off, she waves,
dying to tell me her latest goss.

She gathers her skirts and runs barefoot
through dried mud to meet me.

I feel a sharp contraction in my chest
for the carefree days of childhood.

Her once mousy, greasy crop, long grown out,
is swept into a glossy chignon,

her urchin's scrawny face fleshed out
with pink-flushed cheeks, her upturned nose

is chic rather than snub now,
her small soft mouth devoid of the sores

that plagued her childhood; taller than I,
she has gone from scruffy rag doll

to exquisite porcelain one.
She ushers me into the small lounge,

a low-ceilinged affair, stained
with the brown patches of lantern smoke.

'Come, let's take grape juice. Everyone's out.
Cato is off collaring tax-evaders at some

unpronounceable place in the bush
called Durovigutum, the nanny

has taken the grubs to the baths, the serfs
are out on errands. It is freedom time.'

I follow a ripe bruise at the nape
of her creamy neck, a little darker

than her lilac, low-cut, sleeveless tunica.
'So what's new and exciting?' I ask, knowing

that mundanity is anathema to her,
that she thrives on drama and subterfuge,

that I always followed her lead
when we were hoola-hooping brats,

getting into scrapes when other kids
taunted her with:

Albaleta Skeleta! or *Fester Features!*
'Guess what?' she replies, as usual, pausing,

forcing me into the ritual of:
'You know I can't guess, so cut out

the preamble and shoot from the hip, bay-bee!'
'Let's put it this way.' She reclines

in her wicker chair (a ladylike gesture),
then crosses her legs on its green linen cushion

into Lotus Position (a ragamuffin's one),
puts on a very received pronunciation accent:

'I have of late added to my list of amores.
Remember Sallust, the governor's secretary?'

'Or lackey, depending on your p.o.v.,' I replied.
She tutted but her pewter-goblet eyes

glistened with mischief.
'Here last night, late last night, in fact,

so late it was morning when he left.'
I tried to feign shock but this *was* predictable.

'Hence the lovebite, you slapper you!'
'A very adventurous lover, Zuleika,

reaching parts that a certain tax-collector
dare not explore. Let's just say

that my nickname for him is Donkey.'
'When the old man sees *that* . . .' I pointed

at the blossoming flower on her neck.
'Oh, he's away for five days and it'll be gone

by the time he comes waltzing in here
with his purse jangling with non-declarable

coins donated to Cato & Co.
by terrified victims who've been caught

fiddling their accounts.
Though I tell him that he and his gangster

colleagues had better watch it,
there might just be another Boudicca

out there ready to string 'em up and burn
the towns down.' She leant forward.

I was her only confidante in a town
where gossip spread like sewer rats.

'Horace!' she whispered triumphantly.
'You what?' I replied. I'd heard the first time.

'Horace! The actor. The *famous* actor.'
'You mean *the* Horace?' I teased.

'The one and only,' she replied.
'Wow! So you mean Horace the *actor*?'

She sighed impatiently.
'Not Horace the poet, then?'

She was about to hit me.
'Last Wednesday!'

I threw back my head and laughed.
I'd lost count of the ensuing break-up dramas:

The bastard! The dog! The two-timing rat!
How could he do this to me? Never
trust a man with a moustache, a beard,
blue eyes, green eyes, black eyes, buck teeth,
gap teeth, small teeth, white teeth, brown teeth,
yellow teeth, pigeon toes, duck feet,
bandy legs, knock-knees, short legs,
long legs, fat legs, hairy legs, hairless legs,
oh, but I was so in love with him,
how dare he dump me when I could
have dumped him first! I'll never
ever get over him or him or him or him
or him (or occasionally her) or him or him
or him or him, that's it! No more lovers,
not in this lifetime or the next, nope,
nevernevernevernevernevernever . . . .

'Do you mean never again?' I ventured,
wondering when she was going to learn

her lesson, that sex and love
were synonymous to her, so, for all her

'give it up girls' theorems, she couldn't get laid
without falling in love and getting hurt,

most of the fellas she went with only
wanted one thing, and those that didn't

she saw off. It was an addiction,
to the highs, to the lows, to the routes

towards both – but I kept my thoughts to myself.
I wasn't exactly an example of happily married bliss.

'Yes, I mean never again.'
'Oh, that's what I thought you meant.'

She'd give me a quizzical look,
too wrapped up in her one-act drama

to get my silly attempt at humour.
'Of course Hortensius is around,

but he'll bugger off soon, keeps pressurizing
me with *You Alba, Me Husband No. 2* rubbish.

As if I'd divorce Cato for a florist
and live in a tower block at Tower Hill.'

Alba caught Cato after fluttering her lashes
at his tailor-made cloaks every time

he came into the shop to buy a hamster
or squirrel for dinner. He wooed her parents

with gifts, flowers and an upwardly mobile
lifestyle for their daughter.

Now she was the mother of three baby girls:
twins and a solo act.

'Hope I'll give him a boy next time,
then I can stop breeding. What about you?'

Her tone was almost accusatory.
'When are you going extramarital?

You don't know what you're missing,
the whole town is at it.'

'Yes, but sex has always been an ordeal
for me, Alba. I'm used to it now,

but I can't say I really dig it.
I think I've got a libido, deep down.'

I'd wanted to talk about this for a long time.
It had been bothering me.

'You see, I discovered sex before desire.
At the age I married desire meant dreaming

about how to steal sweet cakes
without Mum catching me. Now, you married

a man you liked, therefore discovered sex
with desire. Big difference.'

Alba shook her head.
'My, my, we have been spending

a lot of time alone, haven't we?
Or reading too many books, I suspect.

Or are you on something?
Been eating those mushroom fritters again?

I don't know, give a girl an education
and life becomes much too complicated.

You're going too deep when the answer
is simple, YOU NEED A GOOD SHAG!'

She was on a roll – in future
I'd keep my thoughts to myself.

'You're every man's wet dream.
They'd be queuing up if a dusky bird

like you went on the extramarital market.
I could find you a man like that!'

She clicked her fingers.
'I know, I know,' I said curtly, looking

behind her at the wall which she'd crudely
painted with Bacchus and Ariadne.

Her perspective was all skew-whiff
and Ariadne appeared to have more bloody

body hair than Bacchus.
I could do better than that. Yet I sometimes

felt so inadequate with her,
so affronted by her ability to enrich

what could have been a humdrum existence.
Her exuberance showed me I'd lost mine.

I was supposed to have it all, not her.
I was the *It Girl.*

'Look at me!' She flung herself at my feet,
grabbed my ankles, stared up with a firey

intensity (*such* a drama queen).
Whenever I went introspective,

she got melodramatic, to put herself
at the centre again.

'Do you want a lover?'
'Why do you have to be so OTT?

Sit down and talk like a normal person.'
She glared at me. I ummed and ahhed,

twisting my neck like a horse straining
at the reins. She pinched my calves.

'I repeat, do . . . you . . . want . . . a . . . lover?'
Now her lips were over-articulating furiously

as if talking to someone deaf, dim or unable
to speak our lingo. I had to shut her up.

'Yes', I replied into my chin, almost inaudibly,
not sure that I did.

'Good! That's the first step.'
She let go of my legs, rolled over

on to her stomach, kicked her legs
into the air behind her, crossed them over,

and continued, obviously excited.
'Male, female, hermaphrodite, eunuch or beast?'

(We'd all heard stories about sheep-shaggers
in the nether regions of Britannia.)

'Male,' I said adamantly. 'Fully equipped.'
'Good! We'll work on it together. I mean

what does Felix expect?
You're still a teenager. Self-service? Bor-ing!

Yet he goes off to his German bints.
But I won't start on that one.

By the way, Zuleika, you're spreading
and you're not even pregnant.'

'I'll never fall pregnant for him, Alba.
I just know it, always have. I probably

can't anyway, he ruined me before I was ready.
He doesn't seem to care,

he's got her and all their blonde sproglets.'
'Fret not thyself over that one.

If I had a choice, I'd not have kids.
I should rename my twins Ball and Chain.

Now Zee, get a personal trainer,
lift some dumb-bells like everyone else,

or go to the gym. Your value's up
but you've got to maintain it. And by the way,

your frock's lovely, but haven't you heard?
Red is the new orange.

Now let me see to some grape juice.'
Rising in what appeared to be one movement

like a cat, she grabbed a chunk of flesh
from my waist.

'Gerrof!' I slapped her arm.
She glided towards the door. I shouted out,

'No! Felix isn't Cato, he'd never allow it.'
She affected a weary exasperation.

'Cato doesn't *like* it. He turns a blind eye.
So long as I fulfil my marital duties

in *every* department he lets it go,
otherwise he knows full well, I will go.'

'You would leave Cato?' This was new to me.
'If I had to.'

'How would you live?'
'What are parents for?'

'What about the girls, you'll lose them.'
'No one imprisons me. I'm not you.'

She swept out of the room.

* * *

I didn't want to go straight home.
I took the river path all the way to the docks,

picked up some scallops and oysters,
laid out on cabbage leaves,

from Thorsten's Fish Emporium.
Thorsten, a Saxon fishmonger, wore his pure

blond hair in a long ponytail, sported
a goatee, had always been good

to me years ago, with a wink and a discount,
even now when he knew I was loaded.

I looked into his kindly face, still ruddy
from years at sea. He was a bachelor too,

with no reputation for womanizing.
What would it be like to see him on top of me?

To have someone respect the *Handle with Care*
signs written all over my body, to look

into a sweating face that sought my pleasure
as much as it expressed its own. Thorsten?

'Is anyting ve matter, sveetard?' he asked,
in his strange, deep, sing-song accent.

Blood rushed to my cheeks, I hurried
back to my sedan without saying goodbye.

The city was smouldering, the docks
would stay busy until late.

I wanted its noise to drown out my own.
I had spent a lifetime avoiding

Alba's timely arrows of insight. Damn it,
she was so often right.

But was a lover really the answer?
It may be Alba's cure-all but I needed more,

I needed a raison d'être to make my mark.
I'd been working hard on my poetry,

I would work harder, yes, harder,
I would devote my every spare moment to it,

which meant most hours in any given day.
The storehouses and shops were packed.

London Bridge was a constant flow of oxen
pulling carts of farm produce from Southwark;

some soldiers rode in front of them, helmets
with red bristles, rectangular, red shields,

jackets glinting silver, their horses
visible through the crossed wooden

fencing, squashing everyone else to the sides;
trading ships were coming in, later fishing

boats would arrive, lanterns bobbing
on the waves; a store was selling glass

vases for flowers. I called out 'Quantum est?'
then stopped myself. What for?

I had bought a load, most of them unused.
Was I an idle-rich matrona after all?

A pathological comfort-buyer?
Barrels were being rolled off a barge

by burly stevedores in brown sacking
tunics and thick leather belts, or topless,

wearing skirts, every other word an expletive;
a pack of wild scabby dogs charged

on to the quay yelping at the thick legs
of sailors coming ashore in droves.

The Fisherman's Tavern was packed
with a drunken crowd of off-duty seamen,

displaying biceps with naked women tattoos:

I Luv Mei Ling
  Zindiwe IV Me
    Yazmin, Mi Numero Uno Futuo
      Doris: Mi & Tu: IV Ever II Gether

They were singing a raucous off-key
round of improvised sea shanties:

Row, row, row your boat
gently down the stream,

merrily, merrily, merrily, merrily
life's no farkin' dream.

The quay stank of fresh and rotten fish,
straw littered the ground. Four raggedy

slave rebels awaited exportation,
sitting against a warehouse wall overseen

by a spear-carrying guard, chained
at the neck and ankles, a sight in vulgar

trousers (unseen in any civilized town),
their legs drawn up towards sunken

bare chests. Builders were constructing
a ship at Blackfriars, a giant

white swan's neck rose before the mast
for good luck. Two fishermen ran along

the quay, carrying eight giant pike
strung on a pole slung across their naked,

scarred, sunburnt shoulders.
I had reached the wall; beyond lay

the River Fleet and beyond that the bush.
I about-turned, went back

down Lower Thames Street,
approached the Governor's Palace,

where I'd often dined with Felix at feasts
that lasted eight hours; attendants

kept busy sponging vomit off the floor
and furnishings, when the Right Honourables

stuck perfumed feathers
down their gullets, or, in the words of Juvenal,

the guests soused the floor
with the washings of their insides.

I took a left up the Walbrook, suddenly
ordered the men to stop.

It had been years, but I would walk
the rest of the way home.

A QUIET BEDTIME VOICE

Her head
comes apart in two sections,

a fringe
with ringlets, plaited cone at the back, air

passes over newly naked
curls, moulded

to her face like a black
cooking pot, white

chalk is carefully wiped
off, dregs of vino, burnt

wood smeared
on to oily cloth, she

can see Zuleika now,
cormorant's wings sweep away

from wide cheekbones, jet
nostrils,

lips like bruised plums,
I am the deepest

of them all,
my amber necklace

is unclasped, gold
swan earrings slid out,

oval brooch
unpinned so my gown

slips off, delicate
fingers massage my head, skin rolls

away
from my mind, the day is over,

space, in between, tingles,
fingers uproot

the tangle
of vines in my shoulders, I

recline
into sighing breasts, Valeria

massages my fingers,
which ones are mine?

Aemilia
leans over from behind,

Madam is sae blue,
sotto voce in my ear,

Madam is sae blue,
her lips whisper-brush my neck,

I shoot wide open, my hands grab
the dressing table

to steady,
I am too often alone,

these wretched girls will play me
like a lyre.

CUMULONIMBUS
(or, It's That Time of the Month Again)

Wind, I feel you stir this blazing
summer night. This empty roof,
this sleeping town, this great stone wall
which circummures us.
I have never left its gates. What *is* out there?
Damn you, Jupiter. My womb is stuffed
with shifting cumulus, sky presses
down on my thoughts like the lid
of a lead coffin and I shrug my silken
nightie to the ground. Bring me
showers, make my red dye come,
wet these cupped offerings, swollen cones,
sore with ova, aroused with revolving thumbs. Let
the sky crack with silver. Let
me hear thunder. Let
me sleep this terrible, naked night.

V

ZULEIKA GOES TO THE THEATRE

The emperor was in town
and some politicos were staging a show

to suck up to him. Valeria and Aemilia
adorned me beautifully and I wore

my favourite wig, which I'd bought
off an Arabian girl who was waiting tables

at a take-away caff in Bond Court.
It ran black and thick to her buttocks.

Aemilia cut if off there and then
and took it straight to my wig-maker

in Threadneedle Street. Now it's piled up
in intricate plaits and twists

with ivory combs and jangling hairpins
guaranteed to make ears prick up

upon my arrival anywhere. Felix left
three weeks ago. Dad sent me a theatre ticket –

he makes more of an effort now Catullus
is away at boarding school –

and I was carried through the riotous streets
to the Guildhall Theatre. Riff-raff

were fighting each other to get into the stalls,
the police were forming barricades, people

have been known to murder over seats.
My entourage followed with cushions,

chicken drumsticks, apples, bread,
sauces and an urnful of yellow wine.

The play began, a comoedia featuring
the fool Pappas and the greedy clown Madacus.

It was cheap entertainment for the masses,
it was tiresomely predictable, the audience

predictably boisterous, shouting,
laughing and cussing all around me.

I wasn't in the mood, my mind wandered
inside itself, where it was happiest.

Was this the highlight of my day?
My week? My month? Was this my life?

Then strangely I felt heat on my right cheek,
as if a flaming torch were being held too close.

The emperor was seated on a throne
some distance to my right, surrounded

by the excited hullaballoo of the male hoi polloi,
and I knew without looking

that his desert eyes were roaming over
my voluptuous corpus, my breasts

had become a sensitive second pair of eyes.
I glanced slyly over. I was right.

OBSESSION

His head is full of curls.
He makes my mind a-whirl.
He's big and power-full
With the forearms of a bull.
His eyes are burning coals
That see into my soul.

It wasn't exactly my magnum opus,
but, as I'd never written a love poem

before, I forgave myself, and started again.
I couldn't get the most powerful man on earth

out of my mind. Nor could the town.
It was bursting with *emperana*: gossip-mongers

were pouring into the doctors with lock-jaw,
every social climber had their ladder out,

debutantes were *doing* new frocks and facials,
and every well-to-do matrona was assessing

the boobs and pubes of all eligible daughters
aged ten years upwards.

The town walked with a straight and proud back,
for not since Hadrian built the wall up north

had an emperor deigned to come west.
The city was no longer a minor

provincial backwater but could claim the label
Urbanus, Heartland of Imperium.

What's more, Severus was travelling single
(with only his guard of 2,000

brave and loyal men); the wife,
Julia Domna, aka Mother of the Camp,

had not come *with*, and his courtesan,
Camilla, an aristocrat of thoroughbred

pedigree from Lower Britannia, renowned
as his official camp-bed follower,

was now persona non grata.
Alas, she had passed her sell-by-date.

Poor old Camilla, wandering minstrels
roamed village and town singing cheap

and completely gratuitous ditties
to news-starved plebs about how Camilla

was really no Helen of Troy, tra la la, fiddle di do,
she rather resembled the Horse of Troy,

tra la la, fiddle di do, tra la la, fiddle di oom
pa pa, oom pa pa, that's how it goes,

oom pa pa oom pa pa, everyone knows
that she'd retired to her country estate

where she supervised the growth of parsnips,
trained horses for the equestrian games

and roamed incognito in the woods,
side-saddle on a pony.

DUM VIVIMUS, VIVAMUS
(While We Live, Let Us Live)
OR, BABE TALK

'Whoooah, get *you*!' Venus sat
mock-open-mouthed as I recounted

The Look in great detail
and the passionate love affair that would ensue.

Alba fidgeted on her stool, impatient
to be centre stage again.

'Do you know how many men give me
that look in a single day?'

'I don't want your opinion, Alba, I just want
you to listen. I've never felt this before. It's fate.'

After all, Zuleika does mean 'The Magnificent One'.
'Yes darlin',' Venus cut in, 'you go for it. Wow,

I could be buddies with the future mistress
of Our Sev. Could end up Aunty V

to a bunch of emperitos.'
We were in Mount Venus. The bar was packed

and one of the worst bands in town, Nu Vox,
was playing the latest Latin jazz, badly:

Little Rex on antelope drums,
Prince Mahmood III on the lyre,

Puff Daddy Fabius on the tuba
and Madd Marcia on caterwauling vocals,

wriggling white triangles of flesh in a revealing
black stola made of fishermen's-net,

her dyed green hair spiked up with gluten,
lips smeared with charcoal.

She emitted glass-shattering vibratos
over a fusion of military marching horns,

the drum rolls of a mysterious Celtic cult
and the discordant twang of the harem harp.

Every so often a drunk punter would bash
his fist against his head, jerk shoulders, beat

his breast, stomp a foot and shout out,
Groove on with it. Ah! Ah!

Otherwise – they were completely ignored.
The Babe Triumvirate were in session,

huddled around a corner table, knocking it back.
Rocking her stool, Alba balanced

it on one leg precariously and folded her arms.
'Lissen-up, Zuleika, he'll be having a different

townie tart every night, so get real.'
'It's real to me. Sometimes you just know . . .'

'What's in a look?' she snapped back.
'If I'd've been there, he'd've looked at me too.'

'It wasn't just a *look*. It was like lightning
passing into my body and taking up residence.

This Über-babe is Über-charged, even now.
I'm buzzing. It's like my tits were my eyes,

they responded to *The Look* first.'
Alba sprang forwards, thumped her stool

on to its three legs, flung her arms open.
'He looked at you, for fuck's sake!

Do you think you're the only woman
he eyed up that afternoon?

Don't create an epic poem about it, Zee.'
'Girlfriend needs a doctor,' Venus joined in.

'Is there a doctor in the house?' she called out
into the room, all ultra-camp and sarky.

I mouthed, 'Watch . . . this . . . space.'
'Yes, dear,' Venus replied.

'You have 'im, then I'll have 'im, then Alba'll
have 'im, then the clap'll have 'im. What*ever*.'

Alba pinched her arm playfully,
but I wasn't laughing. Why was I the one

who never got her jollies, the side-kick
whose mantra was *No! You didn't!*

who went home to bed alone or to Felix,
same difference, for sex was tri-annual

these days, but, even as the thoughts surfaced,
I knew it really wasn't in me to screw

around willy-nilly like Alba,
to give myself piecemeal to the masses,

to lose something precious in the process.
'I will have him.'

My voice was quiet, steady.
Alba flung her head back, guffawing

hysterically or scornfully, I wasn't sure.
'He's too old for you!'

Faint spiders' webs were beginning to fan out
from her eyes. I smirked, imperceptively.

'Anyway, since when has age been a deterrent?
And haven't you heard about BDC?

Black Don't Crack. Just look at me and you.'
Venus looked from me to Alba, then vice versa.

'I think you've got some issues
to resolve here, kiddos?'

She beckoned to a barmaid. 'Some more vino
over here. Pronto! And make it *wet*!'

I drank the last of my honey wine, undiluted.
We were all silent and still for a few moments.

'Oh, Mama gets it. Alba's gone green-eyed
'cos Za Za's gone gooey-eyed.

You know what? Call me psychic,
but I think Zuleika's right. It's girlfriend's time.

What do the ancients say?
When the student is ready, the master will appear.

Give me five, Zuky-dot.' We slapped palms.
She turned to Alba, whose bottom lip

was pushed out into a six-year-old's sulk.
Lifting Alba's chin, Venus added softly,

'Get used to it, luv. The tables have turned.'
'Yeah, well, call me Cassandra.'

Then she turned on me:
'You'll be playing with fire.'

'I want to be on fire. I want to burn.
I want to be consumed. I've been dead

since my wedding night. I've been living
inside myself for years, I want to feel

extreme pain and extreme pleasure.
I want to risk death 'cos then I'll risk living,

I want to explode with desire,
I want to be drippy, drippy, happy, happy,

let it be sung from the rooftops,
Zuleika's gonna get some and cuuuuuuu . . . . . !'

I froze, for the room was suddenly silent,
not a cough, chink of goblet, sound of music,

from band, tarts, sailors, judges, firemen,
barmaids, refuse-collectors, stallholders,

accountants, ring-sellers, silk-manipulators,
soldiers, washermen, senators, policemen,

week-enders, part-timers, full-timers, old-timers,
new kids on the block – all had turned

to stare at me. Oh, sheeeeeet!
Coming to my rescue, Venus announced,

'Yes, folks, my girl here writes mighty fine poems
dontchafink. This is the latest.

Let's hear it for Zuleika the Nubian Poet!'
They clapped, unsure at first, then enthusiastically.

Alba grinned, squeezed my shoulder.
'Pax!' she said coquettishly. 'Pax,' I replied,

blowing a kiss from my palm to her.
Venus gave each of us a Herculean hug.

We were happy families again.
'Thanks, Venus,' I said. 'Quick-witted or what.'

'I have to be, it's a matter of survival.
Now you, Miss Self-Pity, have been protected

from the real world. You live
in clouds of comfort, talk to some of the folks

in here and you'll see how hard life is.
This is the underworld, baby.'

'Pain is always relative,' I replied.
Was *beat me up* tattooed on my forehead?

'Anyway! Change of subject.
Your Terence. How are you two getting on?'

Terence was Venus's long-time, big-time beau.
Last I heard it wasn't going well at all at all.

A married lawyer and father of six,
there was no way he was going to escort

Venus in her make-up and high heels
to any office dinners or political balls.

'Oh, he's around, my Tel.
He professes love but he won't act on it.

I remain his secret plaything,
and I'll not never be nuffink else.

Got to admit it. We've sailed the high seas
and now the ship's about to sink.

You know about the Emperor Hadrian, right?
Nearly a hundred years ago he cavorted

around the world with his pretty boy Antinous.
When said lad died prematurely, Hadrian

named a city in Africa after him, erected
over five hundred statues depicting

Cute Lips as various gods;
deified said lad, built a temple for his worship

(still going on today I might add) and so on
and so forthly and so rightly and what have you.

Now I've told Tel this little bit of history
a mille times. Precedent set many moons ago,

my man. Let's go public.
Just tell the trouble & strife

Tuas res tibi habete, in other words:
Keep What's Yours for Yourself

and she's divorced. She moves out, I move in.
But you know what? He's a coward. What is he?

I-G-N-A-V-U-S. Whadoesthatspell?
I won't go on with the charade no more.

Finis and next customer please. Whatever.'
She lifted her goblet, emptied it in one swig.

MISSING PIECES: A PERFECT MATCH

Purple columbine, amaryllis,
lilac cyclamen, yellow chrysanthemum,

a single white orchid twisted with ivy,
all were wrapped in luxurious,

ultra-soft sheets of perfumed cream papyrus,
delivered at dawn courtesy

of the door-to-door service
of *Wild @ Heart*, the trendy 'flower boutique'

on Cannon Street, and, in bold italics,
a parchment note, each time, a word: *Anon.*

And on the fourteenth day,
a spray of three hundred exquisitae red rosae

(the girls and I counted each and every one),
it was pay-back time.

Oh, make me suffer!
Attached, the ancient Sappho poem:

> *If Jove would give the leafy bowers*
> *A queen for all this world of flowers,*
> *The rose would be the choice of Jove*
> *And blush the queen of every grove . . .*

It was simple enough to track me down,
one inquiry would quickly yield

the identity of the black chick
in understated chic sitting in the stalls

at the amphitheatre that afternoon.
Tranio arched a mischievous plucked eyebrow

as he handed over the bouquets
as if he and I were co-conspirators.

Wishful thinking, buster. This was *my* secret.
I'd convinced Felix years ago

that Tranio needed a wife, that as he wasn't exactly
maître d' of the Londinium Charm School,

he would live a happier, longer life,
everyone knew bachelors and widowers

did not last as long as their married
counterparts. I picked my moment.

Felix lay by my side, catching his breath,
oozing satisfaction, his sleepy member

curled up like a giant slug, still dribbling.
'Does he need one, do you think?'

he replied, the very idea clearly new to him.
'But of course,' I purred, wrapping

a firm warm leg around his flubbery waist,
and stroking his dazed, soggy gastropod.

'Everyone needs a one and only.'
I got the go-ahead, drew up a job description

and person spec, sent it to the Sales Manager
at the House of Venalicius plc –

the elite multinational slave-trading agency,
based in marble chambers at Poultry.

They replied by return of messenger
(the des res postcode of EC4 did not go amiss,

methinks), with a list of potential candidates
and quote for services rendered:

20% commission of the total cost of,
to be paid upon delivery. I made several trips

with Tranio to Queen's Wharf
to size up the latest consignments

from all over the empire, as well as native stock.
As they stood on the auction block,

I selected a short list. In no particular order,
my criteria: Beauty. Age. Dispositio.

Curriculum Vitae. References.
I marked them on a scale of one to ten and Mucia

won hands down with a score of 44 out of 50.

Beauty	8
Age	7
Dispositio	9
CV	10
References	10
Total	*44*

A robust, chubby all-rounder with a ready smile
and transferable skills, she had been a cook,

ornatrix and housekeeper with leading
patrician families in Noviomagus.

At twenty, she was pretty enough
to give a middle-aged man palpitations

when stripped to loincloth and brassiere
(Tranio perspired heavily), yet old enough

to handle the oft-displayed fascista tendencies
of our little enslaved dictator.

Stunted reproductions followed soon after:
a girl who still rolled about on her belly,

and a boy already strutting about the villa
on two short legs – rather like his father.

The mutually enamoured couple
could be heard after hours indulging

in horseplay in their whitewashed,
three-roomed bungalow which adjoined

the main house at the back,
built as a fabulous wedding present from –

Felix the Liberalis and I Want the World to See It.
Tranio would, of course,

henceforth be for ever in my debt.
It was collateral, should I ever need it.

VENUS WINKS AT LOVERS' GAMES

Songbird Surprise
was my favourite dish,

and I knew it would be his.
From first sighting

I had imagined
being crushed into the imperiales

purple robes
of Emperor Septimius Severus,

his sword drawn
out of its gold and ruby

scabbard and plunged into me,
ruthlessly.

Oh, sweet death!
We were together,

finally,
in my triclinium,

a lyre-player
in the background,

as we reclined
on sofas, the low marble table

laid out with a little spread,
served in my floral red Samian

crockery: small songbirds
soaked

in asparagus sauce
with quails' eggs, dormice

cooked in honey
and poppy seed, salted fish

with oyster dressing,
my lord, milk-fed snails,

just for you,
fried jellyfish, bear cutlets,

sliced flamingo tongue
marinated in tumeric and clove oil, am

filling my hunger, par-
cooked

courgettes, boiled
whole, sautéed peacock

brains,
melt in my mouth,

you look across, am
stuffed

dates, torn between my teeth, sow's
udders,

lark's tongue in Gaul garlic, spiced
with perfumed peacock

feathers
and peppered

rose petals,
sweet wine cakes to follow, olives

with thyme,
is on our side, all drowned down

with finest African wine.
We were silent, letting

oils drip over lips
and chins, watching each other

lick it up with acrobatic tongues.
He was solid

like a gladiator,
my Libyan, my lover-to-be,

my libidinous warrior,
my belcher,

his black eyes
following the slope

of my shoulders, my shimmering
cerise gown, décolleté,

fastened with sapphire
clasps, set in gold, flattering

my shining bazookers,
the rise and fall,

with each excited breath.
He was in Britannia

waging war, he said, would leave
when the whole of Caledonia

had been taken,
from Hadrian's Wall

to the Antonine Wall
and way up to the North Sea.

His marriage was impossibile,
he said, his wife

had gone from swan
to donkey.

He knew Felix well,
had often dined with him

at his villa in Rome (news to me).
He called me to him,

nibbled my neck, his harsh
bristle scratching

my delicate skin, stuck
his tongue down my ear, making

me squeal, growled,
Are you ready for war?

MY LEGIONARIUS

I like you two ways
either take off your crown of laurels
drop your purple robes
to the floor
and come to me naked
as a man

or dress up.

– ZULEIKA

Real soldiers wear tunics under armour,
my emperor does without.

Stands before me, metal bands
tied with leather straps

over a bull's chest, iron wings
protect shoulders from flying sabres.

I finger your second skin,
my lord, cold, polished, my reflection

cut into strips; your tawny trunks perfumed
with juniper oil,

hard with squeezing the damp flanks
of stallions, dagger gripped

for my forging.
Are you ready for war, soldier?

A centurion's crested helmet and visor,
curve of dramatic bristle.

Like an equus,
you roll your head, lightly brush

my inner thighs, leaving a trail of goose
bumps, and giggles,

then trace the tip of your sword
down the centre

of my torso. Dare I breathe?
Let your route

map a thin red line?
Silver goblets of burgundy vino by my bedside,

to toast the theatre of war.
Close your eyes, you command, a freezing

blade on my flamed cheek, hand around my neck.
I am your hostage.

I am dying. I am dying of your dulcet conquest.
You make my temples drip into my ears,

whisper obscenities,
plant blue and purple flowers

on my barren landscape;
here,

beseige me,
battery-ram my forted gateway,

you archer, stone-slinger, trumpeter,
give it to me, futuo me,

futuo me, my actor-emperor,
I hold

the pumping cheeks that rule the world,
I do. Ditch the empire

on your back,
Septimius,

it is crushing my carriage,
the weight of a soldier trained to march

thirty kilometres a day,
marching for centuries over roads

made with crushed skulls, legions
forming an impregnable walking

tortoiseshell,
on the battlefield, on

your back,
making the whole world Roman.

Vidi, Vici, Veni.
Take off your victory.

I am vanquished already, I can't fight you,
just stab me to death, again and again,

stab me to death, soldier.

POST-COITAL CONSCIOUSNESS

suspended
on feathers we were
borne on wind windows framed azure sky far off silver
wicks flickering
embroidered silk throws
thrown to the ground were crushed indigo and crimson
anemones we did not stir soaked

anonymous limbs sprawled
a brutish arm sweetly

limp on my shoulder
deep breaths inflating his chest lifting
mine melded
chin into moist arc
of thick neck

mid-
summer mid-
night memory blaze

not since
the first months of life
had I felt another complete
myself

I knew
not
where I began

VI

POST-COITAL COLLOQUIUM

'We exist only in the reflection of others.'
I was suddenly feeling very enlightened,

deep, and desperate to impress.
His lips puckered into a naturally

childish pout, reddish-brown, moist,
within kissable reach of mine,

and equally as fleshy. Long lashes, curly
as a newborn's, were at odds with a forehead

fronting a skull of smoothed rock;
two vertical thinking lines crossed

his frowning horizontal ones,
and if thoughts were things,

they would be storm waves, not outside
but crashing inside the cliff face.

I ran a finger down his bristly cheek.
This was as real as it got –

I'd just shagged the bleedin' emperor.
I wanted to scream out of the window,

do a frenzied dance in honour of Venus,
Glorious Queen of Love

(not the Glitzy Glamour Queen, but oh,
if *she* could see me now).

Venus, who sprang from the foam of the sea
(as you do), who was forced to marry Vulcan,

who had finally cast her spell on me.
After all these years, I had discovered

amore nihil mollius nihil violentius:
nothing is tamer or wilder than love.

'Aiwa, this is how we know ourselves,'
he replied, and I realized that each word

he offered the world was coated in certainty:
Yes or No was the language of my leader.

His voice possessed the rumble of a mortal
who will become a god when he dies,

I could already hear him booming down
from Mount Olympus, *I can see you-oo!*

I sat up. 'Who are you, Severus?'
I had discovered the miracle of love-making,

which dissolved the toughest carapace;
yesterday the question

would have been impertinent,
tonight it was simply – intimate.

He sighed. 'I am what I have to be.'
His breath suffused the room

with a sudden gust of melancholia.
'Who I really am is lost.

Was I that boy who went to the Temple of Apollo
and against music of night waves,

made secret offering to find out
if he would one day be imperator?

Whose father said, "Dream and it will manifest."
But when I replied, "Daddums, I *will* be emperor,"

he scoffed, "Are you mad? A Libyan? My son?"
Soon after I read fine words of Virgil,

who is noster maximus poet, of course.'
('Of course,' I echoed, a tad too quickly.)

'*They can because they think they can.*
I spent every night for years

visualizing myself wearing crown of laurels.
When at last time came to wear

what Picts call *Real McCoy,* it was simply
a case of what Gauls call déjà vu.

I had dream, Zuleika, that one day all peoples
on earth would be my subjects,

not just nine thousand k's of Europe,
North Africa and Middle Eastern territory,

but all those far-away tribes
of whom we know little or nothing.

Was I that boy who wrote poems in Punic
about homegrown gods Melqart and Shadrapa,

before he did similar in Greek and Latin?
Was I that boy who discovered that *colonia*

and *great ambition* spelt husband and wife,
but *colonia* and *fulfilled ambition* spelt divorce?

Who at seventeen sailed
down Wadi Leba on naval warship,

past crumbling boulevards, white colonnades,
past purple bougainvillea, and out into harbour,

past my waving familia, past the lighthouse,
past vision of salt caravans of camels

and nomads in the distant desert, traipsing
en route to hinterland to trade

with the kingdoms of the south,
while I headed north into great Mediterranean,

destined for HQ of think-tanks, spin doctors,
banks, commercial hubbub, intelligentsia,

and general razza-mattaza di Roma.'
He paused, arms folded

across his chest, black curls thinning
out as they trailed down to his belly button –

a lumpen warrior's knot.
I sat cross-legged, exposing myself,

what did I have to offer this giant among men
but my body?

He closed his eyes,
trying to recollect events of so long ago.

I wanted to remake my town
with bright stones and glass!

Oh, to fill his pause with my truth,
but Felix's refrain haunted me, still,

from the first days of our marriage –
silentium mulieri praestat ornatum,

silence is a woman's best adornment –
and I wasn't going to blow it tonight.

My own dream had been blown away,
as soon as my father heard it.

My girlish world was all colours and shapes,
a robe with fuschia stripes,

green cat's eyes blazing in a night alley,
the imperial beauty of the basilica.

Poems were meant to fulfil me instead,
but I failed to create pictures

with my words – or did I?
If he took me to Rome, to the desert . . . maybe . . .

His nomadic eyes settled on me,
so tenderly, as if my thoughts

had been spoken, and heard. I wanted to cry.
He stretched languorously, arched his back,

ribcage like the hull of a barge, protruding
through tautened skin.

He raised his muscled brown arms
to the ceiling – a messy old scar ran down

the inside of his left forearm,
like boiled goatskin. I wanted to stroke it.

He folded them behind his head,
cleared his throat. 'On road to omnipotence

I became centurion, senator,
magistratus, people's representative, tribune,

legate and finally governor.'
Pride and defiance infused every word.

'But I returned home often.
Lepcis is colonia, but prosperous one,

our vast olive groves produce world's finest.
That boy is the father of man before you,

who was ridiculed on arrival in Eternal City
because of his thick African accent.

Today he is icon to sixty million subjects
(give or take few hundred thousand),

yet he drinks potion of acidic nectar. Cheers!
To Managing Director of six hundred

squabbling, back-stabbing Board of Directors
running international Firm on Palatine Hill,

including other Africans who supported
that traitorous Tunisian dog, Clodius Albinus;

who became self-styled MD
while Governor of Britannia, committed

hari kari when hemmed in by my troops,
who removed his brain from his bollocks

and I, yes I, personally trampled
on his headless corpse with my stallion

until he was smashed chicken
(fitting end for coward).

Then I had him thrown into the Rhone,
to make nice chicken soup for amphibians.'

He chuckled as if recalling a humorous anecdote,
then his eyes swiftly shifted from ceiling to mine,

and speared me – all metal,
running cold down my spine, then melting,

molten liquid, flowing into the scoop of the bowl
between my hips. He took my hand

(if I could blush), a kitten's paw in a bear's,
rubbed my palm, suddenly dug a nail into it,

bloody hard. I held his gaze,
but flinched inside, flushed.

'Strong-arm tactics respected, worldwide.
Twenty-six senators executed for consulting

astrologer about *my* life expectancy,
five imperators killed year I took over Firm:

Commodus, Pertinax, Julianus, Niger
and Odious Clodius. *Septic Sev,*

they sneer behind my back. I ask you –
should leader be like lamb or lion?'

Somewhere over my left shoulder,
had appeared an audience. All the men

in my life did this, as if their words
were too important for my ears alone.

This was well rehearsed, over and over again
he had justified his position,

and now to me, though he need not.
He flung his arms in the air, shook his head.

'I am tired, Zuleika, tired of barbarians
clawing at my frontiers after good life,

tired of freedom-fighters, secessionists,
revolutionaries, seditious governors,

break-away factions, religious fantasists,
martyrs, spys, pirates and jumped-up

officers plotting to coup d'état me.
I am tired of hearing

Sevva! Sevva! Sevva!   *Out! Out! Out!*

What do we want?   *Freedom!*
When do we want it? Now!

2, 4, 6, 8!
Who should we exterminate?

This nonsense droning on in the distance
when I am trying to have my midday nap.

There are myriad descriptions
for these bastards, though I have just the one.'

He paused, twinkling, cueing me in.
'What's that?' I obliged.

'A pain in the bloody arse, my dear.
You see, I have simple motto:

Give army pay rise and sod everyone else.
Vanquished *will* protest, I do not blame them.

But may best man win.
I see him in my looking glass.

Enough! I am man of few words
and it has been long time

since I gave potted history to stranger.
It is like life flashing before my eyes.'

He closed his, for a second time,
I had ceased momentarily to exist. I rose,

threw on my silver nightgown, the marble
floor cooling my sweaty, sticky feet,

quietly opened the door. Two guards
were stationed outside it, invisible

yet omnipresent, my house
had been overrun by his Illyrian Guard.

I was a spectre, floating past, ostensibly
unnoticed, something yet nothing.

Be honest, Zeeks,
for all your pathetic poetic pretensions,

you're jus' a likkle housewife,
and to coin a phrase from Venus the Penis,

you'll not never be nuffink else.
I returned with a flagon of Dom Falernum

poured each of us a goblet.
'This,' he announced, alert again,

'is best sparkling vinum in the world.
Bubbles come from must pressed

from withered Ethiopian grapes, wine
is sealed in terracotta amphorae, stored

underground close to cold-water streams.
So you see, my dear, this is not plonk.

I bring only best gifts for such charming girl.'
'Cheers! Here's to longevity,' I toasted,

raising my goblet.
'Ah!' he exclaimed.

'Life and death. Who is winner?
Why can't Caledonians surrender?

I have only penetrated to Moray Firth,
morale is low, my soldiers hate the cold.

I *will* have Scotland. All ginger-heads
will come under my jurisdiction,

but they are bellicose buggers, have resisted
for two hundred years, are worse

than those bible-bashers in the east –
we are the chosen ones and thou shalt not

or you'll burn in hell unless you pray
to our three-for-the-price-of-one prophet.

You stamp out one lot, another pops up.
I am their ill wind. Only death will curtail me.'

He suddenly turned his back to me,
curled into a tight ball, a soft, maudlin voice

emerged, almost melodramatic:
'If I should die, think only this of me, Zuleika,

there's a corner somewhere deep
in Caledonia that is for ever Libya.'

Two toms hissed outside the window,
a barking pack of dogs raced

through the streets, way off I heard
the hypnotic drums of an all-night ritual,

the first cock crowed by the stream.
'What's the matter?' I asked, pressing

myself into his back.
'We believe in the stars in Africa,

and omens. Before I left for Britannia,
the stars said I will never return home.

Up north, an Ethiop with legion of Moors
at Hadrian's Wall waved garland

of cypress boughs at me.
It is terrible luck. He laughed in my face:

*You have overthrown all things, conquered
all things, now be a conquering god.*

Later I was in town to make offering
at Temple of Mithras, more Ethiops

were brought for sacrifice.
Get them away, I shouted. *Bad omen!*'

I slipped an arm around his hot midriff,
his body solid; I had never felt such quiet

physical power, unlike Felix,
who was like a sack of luke-warm water

that shifted to another spot
when pressure was applied.

'Am I not the deepest of them all?' I whispered.
He turned around, wrapped me

in his legs and arms like a warm bundle.
'You are pulcherrima babe.

You bring good luck.'
He rubbed his chin into the groove of my neck,

placed a hand on each of my breasts,
I felt my nipples heat up, grow slowly

erect in his palms. I looked beyond
the window, blue was gradually replacing

black, the stars had faded away, the full
moon was tinged with a translucent glow

that sent an eerie light into the room,
casting a shadow on us both.

THE LANGUAGE OF LOVE (I)

'My beautiful anomaly, who are you?
Nubian, yet not. Woman, yet not?'

We lay listening to our breath as if still lying
on the banks of the Watling Stream

the night before, unable to sleep in the heat,
now oblivious to morning,

which emitted thin lines of brilliant light
through the shutters of the window

and on to the scenic walls of my cubiculum.
'I'm just me,' I replied, wishing

I had a great sob story to relate –
how I was abandoned as a child, ending up

marrying my old man, killing the old girl,
and was about to gouge out my eyes,

when the imperator charged up on a white stallion.
'I write poetry, that's all,' I half mumbled,

thinking, don't ask me to recite. No way.
'Julia too enjoys the finer arts!' he enthused.

Excuse me? Did I ask after the other half?
'She amuses herself with brat-pack

of luvvies for whom she is muse, favours
dishevelled boys in baggy tunicas,

who depict her nude in paintings and poems,
who graffiti *Vivat L'Revolution Y'All*

on the ghetto walls of Rome, then go home
to their parents' villas on Esquiline Hill,

with fifteen bathing chambers.
What can I do?

She will have her playthings and so do I.'
He leaned over, kissed my forehead,

traced my soft open lips with his,
leaving his morning breath mingling in mine.

'Is that all I am?' I asked, thinking,
there's nothing like a post-coital heart-to-heart

to put a girl in her place.
She was old, of that I could gloat,

she would be no match for youth and beauty.
The problem was, neither he nor she

knew there was a contest to be won.
'Perhaps not. I am rarely so candid

with all my women. Julia and I have good
understanding, she is my loyal companion,

but not my keeper, nor I hers.
I am what they call New Man, we follow

popular formula: *To Live Your Own Life.*'
All my women? Admit it, girl, you're one

of the many, not his one and only. Get real.
'But after first five years there are no surprises,

to second-guess opponent is essential,
but predictable wife? What can I do?

I am Sagittarius. She is Taurus.
I am swashbuckler, not couch turnip.

My sons are Aries and Scorpio.
Ah, my sons!' He shook his head.

Your wife is predictable? Then I will be zany,
exciting and spontaneous (for starters).

'Tell me about them.'
'They are alcoholic, despise each other,

abuse boys, embezzle funds, beat women,
hobnob with strippers and charioteers

and spend all day at the races.
What can you do when it is flesh and blood?

Can you feed them to cage of lions?
Can you pull out their fingernails one by one?

Geta is his mother's favourite,
Caracalla is mine, but he prances around

in blond wigs and Germania-style cloaks.
What can I do?

I am respectable, workaholic military man.
I keep them near me and under manners.'

How could your wife produce such wasters!
So it was Julia the Understanding One,

which meant I was just a charming new toy.
If she tried to rein him in, issued ultimatums,

he'd flee into my arms, wouldn't he?
What could I do?

His first wife, Paccia Mariana,
had died after ten years without issue.

'A local girl with intellectual catatonia.
She had no interest in machinations

of government and I none in beauty salons,
gossip and haute couture.'

('How terrible,' I had interjected.)
'You are too clever. I talk but you are silent.

What does life offer you, strange creature?'
When did anyone *ever* ask?

'I'm a nobody wanting to be a somebody.
I was born in this town, but I've never been outside.

I blame my parents, refugees from the Sudan.
This was the first place they felt safe,

so they never left.'
'What of Felix?'

We would of course come to that.
I sought the deceptively light tone that betrayed

the feeling I hoped to recognize: jealousy.
Instead it was casually dismissive,

this was a man who knew his place
in the order of things.

'What is there to say?'
There was too much to say,

but years ago I stopped reflecting
on my marriage, if I opened the lid

of that particular Pandora's box,
who knows what I might find.

'Like you, Felix is somewhat peripatetic,
though he never takes me *with*.

He wants this to be my world – little birdie
in a gilded cage, waiting for her master

to come home – and sing for him.
I have always been somewhat decorative.

Year ago he promised to take me
to his holiday villa in the Bay of Neapolis,

before the act of offering was replaced
with the belief that I was grateful for my lot.

My husband is a mind reader, of course.'
'Of course!' Severus laughed.

'My little minx is mistress of sarcasm!
What other surprises are in store for me?'

'Hang around and you'll find out, buster,'
slipped out of my mouth

before my mind shut its trapdoor.
'I intend to,' he replied, clearly delighted.

I could be cheeky with him, I realized, indeed
he even liked it. I was now on a roll.

'Anyway, that's where he summers
with his concubitch, blonde bratlets,

and other charming members
of the venerated House of Felix, or is it venereal?'

In truth it was I who felt like the concubine.
'Ursula.'

Now I knew her name. Finally.
'You know her?'

Once it became clear Felix would never speak
of her, or his children, I gave up all hope

of ever knowing my husband.
She was the shadow that trailed him.

He wanted my everything but only offered
bits of himself, the Londinium portion,

where he spends but three months a year.
'What is she like?'

After so many years, to finally know.
'Not like you.'

'You are too tactful. I want to know.'
'If you insist. Her face is scarred with smallpox pits,

she has black teeth, those that are left,
a moustache and she is completely bald, of course.'

'Very funny, big man,' I chuckled.
I pinched his side, releasing boyish giggles.

'No! You have found my Achilles heel.'
'Good!' I shouted, prodding mercilessly.

'If you insist! If you insist!
Ursula is beautiful in that aquiline

Northern way, so colourless her features
almost blur into each other.

She plays harp and trummel, she sings,
she describes herself as great tragedian,

though among thespians her histrionics
and high-pitched delivery are considered absurd.

She circles Felix at official functions
like white mountain lion, ready to attack

any woman who shows too much décolleté.
Do you want to hear more?'

I had heard enough.
I felt a tantrum coming on, it had been a while,

and not yet tested on my new lover.
'But you are much more astonishing find.

You are my sweet pulcherrima babe.'
'Of course! You big appeaser!'

'Do I need to lie? Have I chosen her or you?
On the other hand I have another motto:

Candida me capiet; capiet me flava puella.
I'm a sucker for a blonde – and a brunette!'

I slapped his arm playfully.
'What of her children?'

'Five boys.'
Now it was my turn to look away.

Why should I care? He showed me he did,
pulled me towards him, squeezed my face

between his hands, forcing me to look
straight into him, his voice strangely urgent.

'I will take you out of city, many times.
We will go down river to the amphitheatre

in Greenwich; we will follow River Westbourne
from Hyde Park to the jungle of Notting Hill,

camp out, have barbecue and if you are lucky'
– he winked at me – 'play slap and tickle.'

Then his voice sank, melancholic again,
he was the seasons rolled into minutes.

'We must savour every moment together.
Carpe diem, Zuleika.' Our cheeks touched.

'Carpe diem,' I added.
'Who knows what tomorrow will bring.'

THE LANGUAGE OF LOVE (II)

After you have emptied yourself
of all the wars you have fought;
after you have shuddered and roared
and collapsed on top of me, sobbing,
your snores do not reverberate on my spine,
nor do you offer me your back, cold.

Always you ask who I am.
'What do you dream, carissima?'
your head heavy upon my breast.
'To be with you,' I quietly reply.
'To leave a whisper of myself in the world,
my ghost, a magna opera of words.'

I feel the sweep of your lash on my skin,
for my boy slips inside himself again,
to return to his core, his composure,
and I am left rowing with his legions inside,
a galley on a barren horizon,
when the battle is finally over.

AMARI ALIQUID
(Some Touch of Bitterness)

You come, you go,
some nights you stay

to shoot pearl drops into my navel
and marvel at childless skin.

I emerge from clouds,
sticky with fallen issue, to mute

spear-carrying guards,
and a house full of hushed slaves.

Vale, Zuleika. You stride away,
a palm-less wave, and I know

that to ask for more,
is to lose you.

VII

ZULEIKA'S TRIP TO THE AMPHITHEATRE

> The Gorgeous Sev and I
> sailed down the Thames
>
> early one morning
> just as the sun rose o'er Londinium.
>
> It was our first hot date,
> we fed each other grapes,
>
> as we wafted south towards
> the forests of Greenwich.
>
> – ZULEIKA

A flotilla of barges left London Bridge
amidst much trumpeting fanfare, topped

and tailed by man-o'-wars and flanked
by cavalry outriders, who appeared

intermittently on the narrow paths
in between the foliage of the banks.

Severus sailed up ahead on the imperial barge,
long purple ribbons flapping

from the awning above
as he reclined on a couch and held court

with several senior sycophants
who sat fawning before him on the poop deck.

Going out with My Guy, I now realized,
meant there would be no splashy frolics

in our birthday suits, no bit-of-the-other
in the bushes, no stroll hand-in-hand

amongst the daisies while we gazed
into each other's dewy mi' amore eyes.

I would be nowhere near him, let alone
enjoy a good neck-twisting, jaw-aching,

lip-bruising, saliva-slurping snog.
Mistress Invisibilis had been assigned

a barge some distance behind,
with top-ranking wives who knew Felix well,

whose thinned raised eyebrows
and supercilious smirks begged the question:

How on earth did *Illa Bella Negreeta!*
manage to cadge a lift

with the imperial entourage
when the better half was off on an expeditio?

I was just working myself up to snap
at Valeria or Aemilia or to slap them, even,

when I clocked a young harpist sitting
in the V of the stern of his boat, wearing

a pastel-pink micro-mini
(usually the attire of ladies nocturnae,

excuse me) and exposing long shapely legs
right up to her crabby puny.

Her pale oval face, meanwhile, affected
the demure innocens of a Vestal Virgin,

while her thighs opened and closed
as rapidly as the flapping wings of a bird.

A fire ignited in my toes, soared
through my body, devoured my intestines,

heart and vocal cords, until it reached
my brain, where it stayed, roaring.

The plucking bitch! I closed my eyes.
I visualized. She stands. A squall arises.

She loses balance, topples into the river,
reveals a pastel-pink batty pitted

with festering sores, and the Thames
(magically metamorphosed into the Nile)

is alive with water buffalo, alligators, hippos
and an extended family of stingrays.

How *dare* she encroach. Bloody Harpy!
I *would* have words with him – a decision

that sensibly died as soon as it was born.
Was he attracted to her?

Was I just a flingette?
Was to love someone also to fear rejection?

A-M-O-R. It was tattooed on the fingers
of drunken machistos who loitered

outside bars and wolf-whistled at cute
young chicks, whilst grabbing their dicks,

pursing their lips and gyrating their hips;
it was what Alba went on about so much

that no one listened any more,
it was what my parents showed my brother,

what I'd never heard from the mouth of Felix,
and what Venus yearned for. A-M-O-R.

In the words of noster maximus poeta, yeah,
Improbe amor, quid non mortalia pectora cogis?

Oh, cruel love, to what extremes do you
not drive our human hearts?

I flung myself back on to clouds
of soft golden cushions, remembered

the nights crushed in his arms,
took a deep breath and calmed down.

The girls took it in turn to hold a peacock fan
over me, the sun, yet rising, could still

make my chalky face streak with charcoal.
We passed close to the riverbank, and

I stretched out my languid arms, brushed
weeping willow leaves through my fingers.

I saw the round mud huts
which I'd heard existed outside the city;

fields of cabbages, wheat, corn,
flocks of sheep grazing in fields,

wild horses galloping in the hills beyond.
I could breathe without fear of inhaling

human excrementum, or the acrid
clash of perfumes worn to annul it;

yet animal dung, I discovered,
was quite pleasant in its natural habitat.

We passed farmers in brown sacking tunics,
steering oxen and wooden ploughs;

they looked up, mouths agape, heads
slowly swivelled as our water-borne

paraphernalia passed musically downstream.
I floated and rocked, as if in a cradle,

to the music of a wind chime which a slavette
held up at the prow, my silver Valentino

robe with yellow flowery borders
spread lightly about me like air. I was pastoral,

I was a water nymph, I was in the land of the gods,
I was a maiden composed of pure ether,

I was so fucked up to have feared all this.
Ghetto girl or what?

Thanks, Mops. Thanks, Pops.
One of Venus's laconic gems popped

into my head. (She was *so* right.)
'Parents are to blame for everyfink.

*Every*fink, my dee-yah, *every*fink.'
Alba's voice jumped in too, ever the competitor:

'It's water. It's a barge. It's the sun. It's green.
Don't write an epic poem about it, Zee.'

I chuckled softly, wishing they were with.
We rounded a bend in the river, voices rose

in excitement, moving bodies shifted
weight. I opened my eyes,

everyone was standing. I rose, reluctantly,
looked dreamily to where they pointed,

squinting, the sun was now fierce,
and there it was – The Conqueror,

rising out of the tangled roof of forest,
a gargantuan spherical monument,

the likes of which the world west of Gaul
had not seen before. Surely it was one

of the wonders of the world, to stand
head and shoulders with the Parthenon

in Athens, the pyramids of ancient Nubia,
the Colosseum in Rome, embodying

the very ethos of empire: to conquer.
It was many storeys of stone high,

which had been quarried in deepest Kent
and transported upriver on barges; several

arched entrances circumnavigated its base,
blocked with people scrambling to get in.

Londinium was too small for such an edifice, so
the powers-that-be decided on Greenwich,

which would one day form
the southernmost boundary of the city,

from the River Fleet to the River Ravensbourne;
beyond that lay the marshy saltings

and impenetrable swamps of Thamesmead.
To its left lay several low-lying concrete

buildings, with a sign that announced
THE MITHRAS GLADIATORS TRAINING ACADEMIA.

A road cut through the forest from the north,
farmed land either side, carriages

and riders on horseback charged down it,
leaving clouds of dust and heat haze.

We moored to the sound of a heralding trumpet.
I was helped on to the banks,

lifted my skirts and was carried by sedan
over the mud. I had arrived.

NULLI SECUNDUS
(Second to None)

Severus strode towards the arched
triumphal entrance, his purple Armani toga

flowing behind him like wings,
his back straight, wide, unbreakable;

powerful thigh muscles flexed
over chunky scarred knees,

black lace-up booties crunched on gravel
and I thought, you, my darling arrogant

bastard, are just too damn sexy
for my face, *ta rah-tid!*

Nothing would ever get in his way, no one
could oppose him and survive.

He smashed a bottle of Dom Falernum
against the wall: this was his inaugural visit,

therefore the grand opening of The Conqueror.
He turned to the ecstatic crowds,

his be-ringed fist in a victory salute.
A castrato stepped forward, a slender

young man with earnest grey eyes
and lime-bleached curly-perm, thin legs

blending into his neat beige tunica;
he rubbed his hands nervously, clearly more

used to reaching a high C in the bushes
or singing for his supper in the baths

or for the Call-a-Castrato agency in Poultry,
which serviced private parties of dubious nature

and religious ceremonies of public ones.
He began to sing the Pater Patriae, fusing

the pure pitch of a pre-pubescent boy
with the emotional potency of a man

whose balls dropped long ago
and have since been well handled.

When he finished, there was reverent applause
as he bowed out, stumbling.

Stuffy formalities over, the crowd burst
into a jubilant round of *Vivat Emperor Sevva!*,

at which point The Severus, smiling indulgently,
raised his right hand to stop the salutations.

Basta! he bellowed,
and, swishing his toga like a toreador,

about-turned through the entrance.
His posse of the great, good and yours truly

followed behind in formal procession,
passing the lengthy stone plaques inscribing

for posterity a list of Britannia's
senior politicos at time of construction.

We entered the grand ceremonial hall,
its cavernous arched ceiling decorated

with vibrant reliefs of gladiator fights;
we moved through a damp-smelling corridor

lit by torches; climbed a stairway;
and, to a roar of fifteen thousand voices,

emerged out of a vomitorium
into the glare of sunlight and on to the podium

which housed the imperial box.
He's with me! I wanted to shout out

(just in case it's not obvious to y'all).
But Mistress Invisibilis was seated

with the other women in the dress circle
exactly ten rows behind The Severus.

I looked up at the clear blue sky above,
the tiers of seats which rose impressively

all around, packed with man, woman and child
in their bright, festive-best outfits;

vomitoria were built into the auditorium,
regurgitating scurrying latecomers;

each entrance had two tan-coloured,
wooden leopards fully stretched either side

on sloping buttresses, as if pouncing
on prey, heads down; the arena

was a giant pale-yellow oval of smooth,
unsullied sand. An orchestra

was positioned on a wooden platform
to my left, protected from the pit

by a bronze balustrade; they were dressed
in white tunicas with blue belts

and played a medley of ambient sounds
interspersed with rabble-rousing, jingoistic stuff

and hypnotic Celtic beats.
At one end, a man played the water organ;

at the other, women were giving it some
on the horn section; in between

were flutes, lutes, trummels, double-pipes,
pan pipes, harps, drums

and a quartet of ponytailed schoolboys
clacking away on castanets.

I found myself humming, shoulders jerking,
until my eyes, overwhelmed by the crowd,

roamed the restful beach of the arena,
registering for the first time the trap doors

around its circumference, the final
destination of our day's entertainment:

hapless beasts, both two-legged and four,
most of whom would exit prone. I shivered.

The Munera was our national sport.
I'd seen the banners, posters, tattoos,

I'd yawned through countless dinners
where the merits of prize fighters

were debated, I'd heard the soapbox eulogies,
the barroom bragging, and studiously

avoided the real thing.
This lot had looked forward to the big match

for weeks, had journeyed for miles,
some had camped outside for days

in goatskin tents or sheepskin sleeping bags;
street-vendors clambered over seats,

chucking up poppy-seed rolls or apples
or chicken drumsticks, catching

coins thrown down and putting
them into pouches whilst moving on.

A chant began to swell in the lower ranks.
Why are we wai'ing! Why are we wai'ing!

Until *Quiescete!* – shouted
by the coppers at the bottom of every tier,

spears at the ready – quickly shut them up.
I felt an overwhelming urge to take my rightful

place as official consort, slip my hand
unobtrusively under his clothes and work him,

watch him struggle to keep a straight face.
No. I would lift his skirts (and mine),

straddle him, send the masses into a frenzy
as I flashed my shiny, black, shimmering arse.

I'd sho nuff go down in history den,
sprawled all over the *Daily Looking Glass*:

ZULEIKA – THE WOMAN WHO SHOCKED A NATION.
It wasn't fair. We hadn't spoken all day.

I wanted recognition, I wanted commitment.
A tantrum stirred in my feet, but I checked myself.

It had only been one month, after all.
Ave Imperator! Morituri te salutant.

We who are about to die, salute thee.
Three hundred men were marched

into the arena by stewards, formed
into rows of thirty, came forward in groups

of ten to kneel before The Severus.
I had expected the famous Über-hunks

with pumped-up biceps and sex-packs,
the preening supertarts who were pursued

by every promiscuous debutante
who fancied a bit of wotless rough,

who were Guests of Honour at feasts,
intimate soirées and in-crowd orgy parties,

who were millionaires if free, and freed if not,
who lived in vulgares villae overstuffed

with Greek reproduction statues
and murals of themselves in heroic poses,

their penes super-enlarged and upstanding,
who were regulars in the news tablet *Ave!*

and were thus idolized by the lower classes,
analysed by the chattering classes

and satirized by the smug classes
in comic sketches at the theatre,

where they appeared as air-heads,
wot 'adn't mastered the lingua Latin proper,

wot didn't know their Horace
from their hors d'oeuvres, and who'd turn up

at the premier of a bowel movement
with their simpering, pretty-babe wives

wot came from the 'amlets of Essex.
But it was not to be.

Few of this merry bunch had diplomas
in Gladiator Moves from the Academia.

Most were from the ranks of old slaves, convicts,
Christians, prisoners of war and the poor

making a bid for solvency and stardom.
There were men whose cheeks

and bare chests had long ago caved in,
and boys who had not the years

to make solid the space between flesh
and bone with hardened muscle.

Tall, small, thin, infirm, it was only when
the ninth row came forward

that I saw that the back row was female,
beast-fodder, several noticeably pregnant.

Ave Imperator! Morituri te salutant.
Circus animals came on as warm-up acts.

Panthers drawing chariots raced
each other around the arena.

A tiger tenderly licked the hairy hand
of its owner. An elephant knelt

before the emperor and traced the word
Yo! in the sand with its trunk; another

carried an Indian boy in orange turban
and cream nappy, who did cartwheels

and handstands on its back. A bald man
put his head inside the mouth of a lion.

Then the real action began. Goaded
by armed stewards, buffaloes were pitted

against rhinos, lions tore apart the limbs
of jaguars, men were pitted against all.

A red cloth waved at a scabby bull,
a limping bear was pummelled with human fists,

a black cloak flung over the head
of a cross-eyed lion, pitchforks plunged

into mottled, striped or plain skin,
and pointed metal in the third eye

of any beast spelt death.
The crowd cheered as the victors

whooped around the arena,
doing silly walks, pulling funny faces.

These were the pros, the blood spilled
not human, pathetic quadrupeds

were worth less to a promoter than a star biped,
who'd entertain for years to come.

Ave Imperator! Morituri te salutant.
Five square iron cages on wheels carrying

five pacing lions were rolled noisily
across the sand by mules. There was a hush

as five naked women were led out of a trapdoor
on the left, chained at the wrists and ankles,

wild-eyed, scraggy-haired, gagged
with white cloth. Each was taken to a cage,

all were heavy with child. I felt a trickle
of moisture crawl over each vertebra

like a spider, I had been sipping some vino,
a mallet began a consistent tapping

against my temple. I recalled
that sometimes these women were smeared

with the semen of bulls and raped by them;
I'd heard it years ago and forgotten it

until now. The amphitheatre was a brazier,
it was too hot to look up at the sky,

the delirious crowds made me dizzy.
I wanted the band to play,

something loud, something heavy metal,
but they were quietly watching

as each woman was pushed into a cage.
I tried to put my eyes out of focus,

to witness and yet not,
as what had been human became chunks

for the butcher's block: raw tenderloin,
breast, brain, liver, heart,

were consumed until the lions, bloated,
vomiting what could not be digested,

surrounded by bloody meat on the bone,
clumps of hair sticking out of mouths,

stretched out on the floor, and slept.
The orchestra came alive, clashing symbols,

bashing drums, the crowd stood
and roared, and I with them,

Encore! Encore!
My tears subverted into blood vessels,

spilled out of ducts,
boiling red drops burnt small holes

into my cheeks, it was the girl
who so long ago had been stillborn

inside the woman, my throat was sore,
my eyes burnt, I screamed so hard

my stomach hurt, I rocked,
I hugged myself, the pitchfork entered

and turned, warm pee burst down my legs.
Encore! Encore! they cried as one.

Again and again and again and again
and each time I woke up,

it was my first night
in the Kingdom of the Dad, Dead, Father?

The music cut out.
Why did you forsake me?

The Grand Opening of The Conqueror
had turned into the Grand Opening

of my fucking Pandora's box –
and not since my wedding night,

had I cried.

ABYSSUS ABYSSUM
(One Depravity Leads to Another)

Ave Imperator! Morituri te salutant.
The living legend had been created

by a sculptor tapping away
for eons until he'd created cheekbones

worthy of the Olympian Atlas.
Instantly recognizable from graffiti art,

scrawled all over the slum walls of the city,
The Eradicator wore but a shoulder pad,

carried but a sword, its haft twinkling
with diamond sparks and topaz lights.

He was one of The Bad Boyz,
reigning champs of the World Wide Games,

the infamous band of glads who toured
the empire knocking out all oppo: Da Rock,

Undertaker, Sly and Son of Ty
(from whom women fled screaming).

To entertain his fans he did a war dance,
shaking his booty in frilly white undies

at the crowd, taunting the oppo, a little weed
whose see-through skin suggested

a hitherto extended stay in a Zero-Star dormitorium
at His Governor's Pleasure, his spindly

body lost in an oversized helmet,
thigh and shin greaves, metal sleeve

and round shield, as he tried to hold
a wooden, silver-tipped spear in one hand,

which suddenly lunged at the living legend,
an unsuccessful act of desperation

and no co-ordination, prompting
an expression of mock fear from our man,

who shouted, 'Ooh, I such a scaredy-cat!'
and then began to wave his sword

rapidly like a wand, entrapping
Little Weed in its dance,

following his shape but not touching,
up and down, over and around.

The orchestra improvised a slow drum roll
as counterpoint to his wizardry.

There would be no fight, I realized,
no mercy ah-beg-you, no thumbs-up

or thumbs-down, as he began to make incisions
on Little Weed's arms, chest, legs, nips

at first, red dots on white, longer strokes,
stripes, L-shaped cuts, shredding,

we knew what we wanted, hungered after it.
Now I understood it all, oh beautiful, terrible pain,

to witness you without my personal suffering,
let us know that we live, let us live!

Little Weed stood, so still, so life-like,
if he dared move, I held my breath,

how much longer, until the flow of life,
snuffed out, on the ground, now you

see him, que será, será, give it to us,
now, give us a little warm death

for the soul, until, spinning his sword
over his head, The Eradicator let out a war cry,

once more into the fray, we gasped,
dear friends, provincials, colonials, mob,

as he offered it to Little Weed's heart,
such a gift, who collapsed instantly,

with a weak cry, and 'twas Morte d'Weed,
alas poor fellow, his wound so deep,

such a sleep, he sleeps, we shouted
with sweet relief, we brought the fucking

house down, fucking brilliant, mate!
Who's the greatest! Who's the greatest!

we chanted, as the bad boy bowed
flamboyantly, ran around the arena brandishing

his excalibur like the Olympic torch,
while two stewards dragged Morte d' Weed

out by his legs, leaving a bloody ribbon
trailing in the sun-drenched sand.

ALL THE EVIL OF THE WORLD LET LOOSE

None of us is guilty,
each of us took part, as limb
was severed from bleeding heart, I lost
my mind
was flung wide open,
found that demons danced inside,
you only know you truly live
when those before you –

of net and spear and sword and shield,
the clash of will
and skills, suspended breath
and disbelief, I was made numb
with the suspense of who will win and who
will – to each of them their fate
was in my thumb,
                    they live
inside me now all that was contained
has come undone.

VIII

THUS ONE MAY GO TO THE STARS

– VIRGIL

The Babe Three were lounging
on couches in my peristylium after a boozy

lunch of stuffed thrush and lentils.
We were limp goddesses, steeped

in lethargy, heady with the scent of jasmine.
This was our eternal summer, the first

for years when every day the gods
bestowed a ceiling of ravishing blue; the town

had shed its wintry self as if for ever,
as if summer's lease

required no yearly repayment.
Our clenched muscles released, our faces

opened, we smiled, no longer turning inward
because omnipresent clouds

pressed down to threaten rain, carriers
of a chill that seeped into our bones

and never left;
but, like the phoenix rising from the ashes

of deadened passions, we were reborn,
or so I thought.

Perhaps it was only I, covered in tingles,
as if his invisible fingers were always roaming

my flesh, his breath the very air around.
We lay as three muses,

so lovely, and so completely intemperate,
and now I had an imagination to inspire,

I would not fade.
Or did the sun shine too fierce upon my head

and create plants from seeds
that should have been left for dead?

How I craved to possess
he who cannot be possessed.

A plaything! A new refrain,
landing like an arrow on my temple

each time I remembered, more potent
than all his sweetest endearments.

All that I am not to him, I will become.
All that I need, he will provide.

Or should I stop drinking at lunch time?
Venus had been delighted by my news.

Alba said he just was using me.
'Come again?' I replied, to which she added,

'It's up to us to protect Zuleika.'
Venus snapped,

'Admit it, Alba, You're I-N-V-I-D-I-O-S-U-S.
You didn't snare the main man, innit.

I mean, omnipotent stallholders? *Excuse me!*'
Ooh, a bit below the purse-pouch, Veen.

But Alba could take on all comers.
'Venus, you're fake, every*fink*, my *dee-yah!*

about you is fake.' She began ticking
them off with her fingers. 'Clothes, voice, boobs . . .'

'Wrong! I'm true to what's inside me.
I allow the real Venus to float to the surface.

An' you sound just like me old man, Jeez!'
She began walking around the courtyard,

dragging her feet in leather flip-flops,
natural brown hair up in a ponytail.

I walked over to the rose bush,
picked off some crisped leaves.

'In case anyone's interested,' I called out, 'I'm

(a) happy
(b) having my assets plundered
(c) been to the countryside
(d) poems are pouring outa me like piss.'

'Glad to hear it.' Venus came up,
plucked a fuschia rose, put it behind her ear,

stamped her feet, clicked imaginary castanets.
'Fink I'll change me name to Carmen.

So when do I get to meet said hunk?'
Greatness would be hers by association.

I diverted: 'I want to be with him . . . for ever.'
Alba joined us, pale blue dress

clinging to ever expanding curves.
She fanned herself, wearily, like she'd lived

to a hundred and was giving us the benefit.
'For ever is a myth. For ever means

I hate you but hide it for the sake of the sprogs
and the security of your spondulicks.'

Like scales, she had to rise
so that I would sink.

The result? To weigh me down
or perhaps balance?

We muses always answered each other
as if in song; the words changed

but underneath the same old tune.
'Don't listen to her, Zuky-dot,' Venus enjoined,

'I believe in for ever. I believe in dreams.
I believe in finding my soul partner,

a life of domestic bliss, then sailing
off to Tranny Hades together.

Oh, to hear from my dearly beloved,
quid nocte cenabimus, carissima,

in other words,
what's for dinner tonight, darling.'

She began to sing, twirling her dress,
she grabbed my waist, we spun, we sung.

There's a place for us,
somewhere a place for us . . .

Alba mock-vomited. 'Slush queens!'
She crossed her arms, stood in a corner,

tapped a foot, aged eight again.
'Let's have a poetry party,' I sang out.

'Life is gloriosa! Zuleika est so felicissima!'
I stopped dancing. Venus flung herself

on to a couch, threw her legs up the back,
exposing three-day-old bristle.

'Tut! Tut!' I pointed at them.
'So?' she said. 'Who's gonna stroke

these Scotch eggs and say gruffly yet tenderly,
Ouch! A little bit prickly tonight, luv.'

'That's why we should have a poetry party.
You'll meet a different calibre of the male species.

I've been scribbling away for years now,
I want exposure. I want recognition.

I want a standing ovation!'
In truth I wanted Severus to hear of my work,

without the agony of seeing his judgement
flicker across a face I was learning to read;

to know of my talent through the acclaim
of an adoring public, to see

I was so much more than just a pretty babe.
'What say you, Albs?'

Alba turned away, not sure whether
to come out of her sulk, then chilling.

'Sorry, Veen, I love you the way you are.'
'Half-hearted apology accepta. What*ever.*'

Alba turned back to me.
'It's a brilliant idea, it's the in-thing,

I've been to loads and this manor is perfect.'
'I didn't mean here.'

'Felix is away, Tranio's your new best friend.
It's huge. It's luxuriosus. It'll be a gas.'

Venus nodded vigorously in agreement.
'Let's make it fancy dress too.

Guests can come as animal, vegetable . . .'
'Or mineral, perhaps?' I interjected. 'Bor-ing!

I was thinking of a recitatio-cum-orgy, actually.
I get to read my poems and the orgy

will pull in the crowds.
The tricky bit is getting poets to appear.'

'Sounds good to me,' Alba replied. 'Venus?'
'Sure, but no worries about an audience.

Everyone wants a laugh, 'specially if it's free.
As for poets, any old chance to show off.

I'll be MC, Master of Cunteries, darlinks.'
'Sorted,' I replied.

'Sorted,' Alba agreed.
'Now Zeeks, ring your ding-a-ling

and order some peppermint rosie lee
and some of that tasty carrot sexton blake,

we've got a happening to organize.'

VERBOSA ORGIA

> Scarce a day has passed wherein we have not been
> entertained with the recital of some poems.
>
> – PLINY JR

Venus gushed over, all towering bouffant
and frou-frou orange gown.

'Ain't never MC'd a recitatio before, Zee,
only the Alternative Miss Londinium

at the Forum and drag nights at the club.
I'm so excited! Aren't you?'

My triclinium had been transformed into a packed
auditorium with rostrum, black drapes,

a sea of cushions and flagons of plonk
served up by Valeria and Aemilia, busy

pretending to avoid slappy-happy palms.
I'd gone for the literary sophisticate look:

floating black cape and three rings
on each hand, which I'd been told

was the least expected of all good poets.
Alba was flitting about in a backless

green frock, homing in on any young male
whose gems appeared genuine.

'Excited? If it means tap dancing teeth
and a cane for a spine – then yes.

I'll recite one poem and I'll go on last.'
I didn't mean to be terse,

but this new cocktail of hope and fear . . .
'Right you are, then, my little diva!'

Venus giggled. 'Now off into the fray!'
She pushed through the audience,

climbed clumsily on to the rostrum,
stood legs apart, arms akimbo.

'Right! Shut the fuck up, you fuckers!
We aim to turn you on wiv verse today,

but keep yer pricks in yer cotton knicks
till the end and poets, none-a-this

I'll bore you for five hours shit.
You've got ten mins each – max –

or I'll set Tranio on to yer an' you'll feel
his daisy roots right up yer kazi.

Say grrrr, Tranio.' 'Grrrr!' Tranio replied,
hitherto cross-armed at the door,

now beaming at the attention.
'Right! First up we have the magnificus!

The singularis! The splendiferous!
The fantasmagoricus Hrrathaghervood!

Give it up for the very real Authentic Pict!'
She jumped up, punched the air. 'Booyakah!'

Hrrathaghervood sprang barefoot
on to the rostum, face dyed blue with woad,

snarling wolf tattooed on his forehead,
ginger dreadlocks down his back.

There're only three groups of fowk I hate,
De Romans who're trying tae thief Scotland,
De Celts who've sold oot tae de Romans,
An de Christians who didnae wint nae bugger
tae enjoy thaimsels . . .

He shook his locks, waved his arms about,
fingers bearing ten spoked rings,

as he strode up and down, shouting.
He finished to a standing ovation,

and comments on how beautifully
he shook his plait-things,

the exotic charm of his Pictish patois,
the symbolism of rings *as* knuckle-duster

and how brilliantly he *did* Anger.
Mesmerized by his voice, overwhelmed

by his stage presence, I had hardly
listened to his utterances, wondering

how I could possibly compete?
Venus clambered back on to the rostrum,

swigging en route and dribbling.
'Give it up one more time for that red-haired

barbarian Hrrathaghervood!'
She blew him a kiss, and winked.

'Come rant and rave at me, bay-bee, anytime!'
Next up was Pomponius Tarquin,

winner of the Governor's Award for poetry,
a stooped old man in a raven-black wig,

who swished his silk cloak disdainfully,
wore twenty rings, two to a finger.

'My new volumen,' he announced,
through Roman nose and pursed lips

(available at the back there for a discount),
'is called *Matter, A Moment.* This first poem

is called 'The Day My Cat Died'.
There are one hundred in the collection,

but I'll read only seventy-five of them now.'
There was a loud collective groan.

Life exists, then life is gone. Such eternal
Questions, did my old predecessors, the great
Philosophers, pose. She was here, now she's not.
It was a grey day, the day my Posy died.

Was I missing something?
I knew his sort, hadn't I married one?

To the patrician I was always less than,
as if my very birth were an aberration.

After the third rendition, the audience
began to talk, two plump middle-aged women

fondled each other's breasts in the front row,
an inebriated group was throwing

papyrus birds at Pomponius, until Venus,
hitherto fluttering her lashes at the Pict

(smiling surprisingly sweetly back at her),
finally noticed and bounced on to the stage.

'Awright, Pompy-baby, get off
or the bulldog'll 'ave yer!'

'But I have not yet finished!' he protested petulantly.
'Oh yes you have!' the audience chorused,

at which point he threw his volumen
at them and stormed out, muttering,

'Margaritas ante porcos! Yes, you heard!
Pearls before swine!'

Afternoon rolled gregariously into evening.
There was Calpurnius Tiro,

the 'mud, plough and sow' poet,
reported to be popular with sheep

and farmers nationwide, unfortunately
there were none in the audience;

Manumittio X, whose every poem began
Take these chains from my heart,

and finished with *I just wanna be free.*
Some told jokes in between their poems,

or just told jokes – they were popular,
as were those who sang and danced.

A gaunt, bald man announced
he was the great-great-great-great-great-great

grandson of God, donned a crown of thorns
and, as blood poured forth down his face, uttereth,

Repent or the Lord will rain
Brimstone and fire,
Thrush and syphilis,
Herpes and gonorrhoea,
Divorce and unwanted pregnancies,
Vaginal warts and blindness
On Sodom . . .

at which point Tranio had him dragged out.
I later heard he'd been duffed up

and left for dead in the street.
Verbosa Orgia had descended into an almighty

piss-up, feel-up and throw-up, the floor
was a pit of writhing flesh, grunts and gasps,

even Valeria and Aemilia were entangled
in a foursome at the back.

Had I given them permission?
I would have words on the morrow!

I felt as sober as a lictor,
the sensible one amidst mayhem,

yet I was supposed to be the Orgy Queen here.
I had sat quietly working myself up,

intimidated by the confidence of the poets
and the intolerance of the audience.

I looked for Venus, who had stopped policing
proceedings long ago, found her

on the Pict's lap, legs splayed either side,
hairy buttocks displayed for all to see.

(Honestly, I'd have to advise the girl.)
I dragged her off her new beau.

'Hello, Shooks, you shtill ere, luv.'
'Whatdyamean? I've not gone on yet!'

'Thash right. Shuch a brave shoul.
Isn't Hroshagurd luvverly. I call 'im Big P.

I fink ahve fallen in love.'
'Lissen-up, just introduce me will you.'

'Okey dokey, me old mate.'
She staggered over to the rostrum.

'Genlmen, the higlight of thish evening
is Zhleika, our very own Nubian princhess,

so SHURRUP AN' SHIT UP!'
She all but fell into the audience and all

but crawled back to Big P's lap.
I looked for Alba, who doubtless owned

some of the limbs sticking out
from the mass of worms in the corner.

My heart felt like it was gonna explode
and land messily on someone's lap.

I put my eyes out of focus, I felt faint, began,

Identity Crisis: Who is she?

Am I the original Nubian princess
From Mother Africa?
Does the Nile run through my blood
In this materfutuo urban jungle
Called Londinium?
Do I feel a sense of lack
Because I am swarthy?
Or am I just a groovy chick
Living in the lap of luxury?
Am I a slave or a slave-owner?
Am I a Londinio or a Nubian?
Will my children be Roman or Nubinettes?
Were my parents vassals or pharaohs?
And who gives a damn!

I found the courage to re-focus my eyes
and saw that the only person listening was Tranio

who nodded encouragingly at me,
in between uncontrollable yawns.

I left the room, for to strip and open
my legs was the only reason to remain.

DUM SPIRO, SPERO
(While There's Life, There's Hope)

'How dare you!' I screeched,
playing the Grand Dame of Londinium,

hands on hips, shoulders hunched, freezing
them in their footsteps as they entered

my cubiculum, sheepishly.
It was the morning after.

My pulsating brain was afloat in alcohol,
the result of six goblets of foul yellow vino

in the sleepless early-morning hours,
for after my show-stopping début,

my soul felt like a hollow bowl
that needed to be quickly filled up.

I had *not* been the star of the show. Factum.
The Authentic Pict clearly was. Factum.

Someone had to pay. Factum.
'Mistress non est very happy!'

'You have brought shame on me,
my husband, my parents, my ancestors.'

I was going to add, Yay!
You vixens will be responsible

for the Fall of the House of Felix,
but stopped myself just in time.

The room was still in subdued lamplight,
for I dared not allow daylight

to assault my tired, bloodshot eyes.
'Is it in your job description to have sex

with my guests? In case you have forgotten,
you are S-E-R-V-A-E. Whadoesthatspell?

Here to serve and obey, not get pissed,
cruise the joint, strip off and copulate

in flagrante delicto. I've a mind to send
you down to the docks to board

the first boat out to Gaul on the morrow,
wearing *lovely* iron necklaces.

By the way, I hear they do give girls regular
check-ups in the army's outposts of Syria.

What have you got to say for yourselves?'
I stared from one to the other.

Both hung their heads in shame (I hoped),
but sensed it could be fury, or perhaps fear?

It was so hard to read beneath the flecking.
Valeria, usually the braver of the two,

by far the plumper, prettier and brainier,
raised her head and started to speak,

but hesitated, closed her pale lips again.
'Well?' I said, as coldly as I could muster,

using Clarissa's RP classes to good effect.
(If I had known then how often

How nunc brown vacca would come in useful.)
Valeria looked to Aemilia for support,

but *she* looked close to tears.
'Madam is waiting,' I said, intoning

just like the late, gladly departed Antistia,
in fact sounding like every magniloqua

matrona I'd ever had the misfortune to meet,
with a little bit of Venus camposity

and the pompousness of Pops thrown in too.
What had I become? But a composite.

'We winted some dafferie, madam.'
'Fun? Is it not fun working for me?'

'Aye,' Valeria replied hastily,
'but nae that sorta dafferie. Tail-toddle, ye ken.'

'You mean you wanted sex?'
She chewed her bottom lip, nervously.

'Aye, there's naethin wrong wi it.'
The blighter, telling *me*.

'I thought you two serviced each other.
Sister to sister. *Such* are the times.'

'What we really wint is to git wed, madam.'
Shock did not register on my face.

'Why? Pray tell.'
''Cause it's what fowk do, isn't it?'

I glared at her. She stared me out.
'We wint to hiv bairns.'

Aemilia piped up at that.
'Aye, bairns. We hiv needs.'

They had never spoken of needs before.
What New Age thing was this?

Then the denarius dropped. Duur!
They'd observed me and my Sev,

and it was giving them silly ideas –
they'd never been inspired

by my sentence to the delectable Felix.
How could I let them marry?

I mean, the Vestal Virgins were just that.
Were they recruited from lustra?

No, they were pure, their devotion to Vesta
guaranteed to be absolute.

I'd have to find two new girls, tour the auctions,
it could take months to train them up.

What would I do without these two?
We'd virtually grown up together.

They kept me sane in this friggin' house.
'What about my needs?'

'You wouldna lose us, madam.
We'd still be yer personal servin' lasses.'

'Thanks for letting me know, Valeria.
My answer is, quite obviously – no.'

'Please, madam, think aboot it, at least.'
I went over to the dresser, sat down,

looked in the hand mirror, sighed.
'We could ax Felix.'

The girl was pushing me over the edge.
I did not turn around,

but watched them in the mirror.
'Felix will defer to me.'

'He'll dae oniething for ye, madam.
He'll even give us oor libertas if ye ax him.'

'From sex to marriage to manumissio –
all in three minutes. Quite remarkable.

Felix will do anything for me?
There is always a price to pay, ye ken.

You will have your libertas when I die,
as you are both well aware.'

They began to cry, hysterically.
'No!' I stood my ground.

'That's not a Y, or an A, but an N.'
'Please! Please!' they begged.

'We cannit gae on like this, we'd raither dee!
We're so non fortunatae.'

Here they were, chucking their pain at me,
as if I were a bloody sewage-collector,

as if I hadn't had a lifetime's worth myself.
They hadn't been thrown into the lion's den

with the likes of ille patronus, had they?
They'd lived the life of bloody O'Reilly

with a domina who'd never beaten them,
dressed them in exquisitus fabrics,

with nay an unkind word in all these years.
Other slaves were no more than sexual

chattels, or worked like mules,
or wore hand-me-downs – I'd dressed

these two in bloody Gucci, for Jove's sake!
Now I am responsible for their needs?

Tears began to fall down my cheeks.
I was supposed to be telling them off,

but they'd turned it round to their advantage.
I thought they were grateful.

They'd been such sweet, quiet girls,
floating around me, never a cross word.

Had I got them so wrong?
I realized I knew jack shit about them:

zilch, nil, nix, naught, niente, nulla.
There was that horror story years ago,

all about Boudicca reincarnate
and heads on spears,

but it was better to dismiss such things.
Life began for the girls when we met

and it had been good to them.
I needed to go and lie down, this day

should really pass by without me in it.
It was Aemilia's turn to make a pitch.

'We miss hame so much. Every nicht
we talk aboot it afore we go to dormio.

We picter everyone, hearken their vices.
We miss de air, de hulls . . .'

'Accept your fate like everyone else.
What we have is all we can hope for.'

Who was I kidding? I never stopped
plotting these days.

'My head feels a thousand times worse.
Bring me the hair of the dog, remove

my make-up, I'm going back to bed.'
'Will ye forethink yer answer, madam?'

'There's nothing to reconsider, Valeria,
and if you continue to pester me

you'll be back in those identity tags,
Hold me lest I flee & return me to my master.

You will remember the early days.
Now stop the bloody whingeing.'

They worked quietly, cleaning my face with oil
and cloth, hands gentle and assured,

as they'd always been, but what I now felt
was pure odium oozing out of every freckled pore

in their bodies. I was the person this world
had created me to be, and so were they,

though who I was becoming,
I was not so sure any more.

Our lives were in the hands of the gods,
though we could tinker with them, if lucky.

If lucky I will end up far away from here,
at my beloved's side, they can come with,

I will need them in a strange land; then
and only then can they marry.

Of this they will know, as and when.
One thing I knew for sure –

I had suddenly become
Public Enemy Numerus Primus. Factum.

POST-MORTEM

'Za Za, you were da bomb.'
Venus landed two smackers on my cheeks.

'Star of the show, girlfriend!'
Alba gave me a body-popping hug.

'Thanks, but that's a bit rich considering
neither of you listened.'

'Oh, but we did,' they replied, looking as pleadingly
earnest as two liars could.

We were in the atrium, two days later.
I moved to the edge of the fountain,

where Medusa spat on my neck.
'No, you didn't.' I hastily wiped away an escaped

tear before others cottoned on and followed.
Venus put an arm around me.

'Sorry. Guilty as charged. I got drunk.'
'Me too,' Alba admitted. 'I was so excited

at being at my first orgy in months.'
'Surely there's more to life than sex?'

I raised a brow, cut an eye at her.
'Such as?'

'Listening to your best friend's first reading?'
She knew not where to look.

You were never going to sit and watch
me be a somebody, were you, Albs?

'Let's forget it. I went on too late.
No one cheered, said I was brilliant

or the Next Big Thing. Nothing.
I've had it with poetry. Finis.

My future lies with Severus, I've decided,
I'm going to make damn sure he marries me.'

Shock instantly replaced grovelling
on their pathetic, humbled mugs.

Venus jumped in: 'Zuleika, that's silly,
poetry's your lifeline, who cares if they don't clap,

it's not about that, it's about the art.'
Eager to change the subject, eh?

'It's about a standing ovation, Venus.
It's not fair, my whole life

has been one long trail of diarrhoea!'
'Are you premenstrual?' Here we go!

Alba's usual catty remark when conversations
got too deep and she wanted to shut me up.

'Oh, don't talk to me about periods,'
Venus exclaimed, shaking her head,

as if they were the bane of her life.
Alba and I, restraining our laughter, shouted

together, 'Shut up!', united again.
Venus took my chin in her hand, her motherly

gesture – she had several.
'A mistress has to be *strategic*, darling.

Ask for nothing, outright, anyway, never complain,
always give it up, take each day as it comes.'

She'd suddenly gone very RP.
'I'm with Veen,' Alba agreed.

'Be cautious. Be clever. Be calculating.'
'Point taken,' I said, thinking, yeah, right,

you two aren't exactly my role models.
I was my own best adviser on this one.

'So, Miss Venus, the Authentic Pict, eh?'
'To be honest, I'm very surprised at you,'

Alba butted in, frowning.
'I thought you wanted Normal.

I thought you wanted Stable.
I thought you wanted Respectable.'

Venus stretched her arms to the sky, the sun
nourishing her glowing face, devoid of slap.

'He's all those things, believe you me.
He's actually a very sweet young man

who wants to settle down.
We're both actors in one sense,

sensitive souls in this cruel, cruel world.
Do you know his real name is Robbie

and that he was born fifty miles south
of the Antonine Wall, so he's not a real Pict.'

It felt right, him and him.
'What's with the posh accent?' I asked.

'Ain't not never 'eard the like before, luv.'
'Actually, Alba was spot on, as usual,

it's time for the real me to come out of the trunk.
I've a skeleton under the bed, girlfriends.

Daddy was a leading senator in Rome,
he owns a massive estate in Camulodunum.

He also heads an important consortium
of loaded east-coast landowners.

I'd love to take Big P to meet the parents.
It's been fifteen years.

We'll hide in the bushes, jump out
when they go for their passata,

give the old bat and old bag heart seizure,
then the only son will inherit. I missed them

for years, you know, sent many an epistula
with the imperial postal service, each one

costing entry into the mysterious world
of my back passage, offering an olive branch

and my address, wherever it was in those days,
er . . . second tree from left outside the Forum

. . . er . . . third boat from bridge on the beach.
Did they reply? Even when I settled?

I'd love to turn their home-on-the-range
into an upmarket health farm,

call it The Steam Palazzo, for the RQN,
Retired Queen's Network, darlings.

I'm truly tiring of inner-city life,
These days I dream about running through fields,

the wind blowing through my wig,
and a buck-naked Big P panting after me

and flinging me down on a bed of buttercups.
Let's get some fresh air, come along.'

We went for a walk down to the river front,
linking arms, Venus in the middle,

our steps easily in rhythm with each other.
Singing loudly, we ignored

the bemused stares of those poor souls
on the docks who still lived in one room

with a bog hole in the corner
and a stove in the middle.

Life could be worse, I suppose.
We are the three amicas!

IX

EVERY LOVER IS A SOLDIER
(Militat Omnis Amans)

– OVID

We had left the city fortress at dawn,
crossing the small bridge over the River Fleet,

startling sleepy young sentries,
trembling hand-across-chest salutes,

our rattling open carriage which you drove,
whipping the rears of four furious stallions,

as you tore ferociously down the Strand,
profile fierce as Pluto, hungry for speed,

addicted to the pulse of battle.
Farmland spread up in hills to the right,

a ghostly, mist-filled Thames to the left,
three hundred armed guards galloping

on horseback, flashing red capes
up ahead, and behind; wagons with our provisions –

without the paraphernalia of state, this time,
the Great Danes and stuffed togas.

I thank you for that.
We climbed the winding path of Haymarket,

arms of trees forming an arbour, emerged
out of the cloud of mist into daylight.

I held on to my seat, as we raced
over the wild sloping grassland of Mayfair,

cut across the wheatfields of Hyde Park,
passed a sleeping hamlet of mud huts

by the Serpentine, followed the lumpen banks
of the River Westbourne, as our cavalcade

edged slowly into the humid jungle
at Bayswater, soldiers up ahead

cutting a path with axes. We entered afternoon,
sunlight began to filter through the trees.

I relaxed in my seat, surprised
by the noisy conversations of insects

and birds tree-hopping, frightened
small hoofs escaping into the undergrowth.

A large black spider,
suspended from a branch by a fragile thread,

almost brushed my face.
I inhaled the dew-soaked earth, damp bark,

wet fronds, a single
blade, wearing an opalescent earring,

at its tip. I offered
my naked, wind-beaten cheeks to the sun –

the humid breath of summer.
We crawled along a tributary, arrived at Notting Hill,

discovered an overgrown clearing
where the jungle swept down at Portobello,

quickly disentangled by our army of sickles.
A large Bedouin tent was erected,

a camp for the soldiers in the woods
who had been stationed at every stage

of our journey, you said, and beyond
to Kensington High and way out to Fulham.

Yay! Such is the burden of omnipotens,
my dear. I went exploring, wolves, bears,

savages were unwelcome visitors
in my mind. I flung them out,

I knew I was safe, here with you,
and three hundred soldiers.

I snapped the stems of forget-me-nots
from the base of a tree, found a raspberry bush,

picked a handful for you,
fed them on to your tongue, one by one.

We sat listlessly under an awning, ordered
flagons of beer, rustic-stylee,

a gong for room service, the air was heavy,
a wild hog roasted slowly on a spit,

basted with garlic and lovage oil,
mingling with the heady aroma of wood smoke.

I deepened my breaths,
you ripped its succulent hide apart

with your hands and proffered
with chunks of bread dipped in garum.

We tore at our feast, starving,
until we could not move,

you lay your lethargic head on my lap,
let the strain drain away.

'Why did you pick me?' I asked,
for I was in the mood for compliments.

'You were like desert girl in Londinium.
So beautiful. I will never see desert again.'

'Don't say that. Of course you will.'
'You cannot argue with science of stars.

Why did you like me?'
What, apart from the obvious, I thought.

Men with power et cetera.
Surely you can't be that naive, our Sev?

But in truth there was more to it.
'I knew you would make my world larger.

It was *so* small, inside and out,
I would discover more of myself through you.

Will you tell me about the Sahara?'
'We call it Bahr-bela-ma, sea without water.

Desert must be respected, it is ruthless.
Yes, worse than emperor, if it is possible.

Early Romans were afraid of desert,
it stopped empire going further south.

Like sky it can be all colours, reds, golds,
purples, black, silver, remarkable, like sky,

and like sky, you can see for ever.
It is colder at night than in Scotland. Yes!

In daytime is sun outside? No, sun is inside you,
and if you have no water, it erupts as blisters,

absorbs all your fluid, until you shrivel up and die.
Sometimes you are in middle of massif,

other times shifting dunes are everywhere,
for desert is always changing, it is rock

which billennia have crushed
into tiny particles of sand.

Sometimes you see salt caravans
of more than 30,000 camels,

stretching for miles.
Salt is sold ounce for ounce for gold.

It is like mirage, when you see something
that is not there. So wonderful.

Sometimes you will find oasis: palm trees,
pools, cash-and-carry shop,

but most of it is barren, a waste land,
then nomads wash in sand, not water.

You cannot imagine how beautiful it is, Zuleika.
Britannia is like pigs' ca ca in comparison.'

He waved a dismissive arm at the jungle,
took his goblet and clinked mine.

'Cheers! To Sahara!'
Then the blue sky quickly filled with thunderheads,

broke over us, lightning shot
out of the forefinger of Jupiter.

And then it rained, it rained et pluviam,
et pluviam et plurimam pluviam.

We ran inside the tent, you lay sprawled
on luxurious burgundy eastern rugs,

as a battalion of iron balls
descended through the leafy canopy

of old oak trees, battered the canvas roof
of our tent. A raven cawed

far off in the distance, a grunting
family of pigs scuttled past, charged

into the bushes,
our vista became splattering mud,

the phalanx of trees on the opposite bank
disappeared,

a hot bronze curtain met the river as vapour,
my fingers

penetrated your bushy hair,
pulled it up in tufts, squeezed the tension

out of your head,
to your quiet, grateful groans.

I untied the Gordian knots in your shoulders
with juniper oil,

pummelled your back
with my fists,

knuckle each vertebrae down to your coccyx,
knead your hard buttocks,

rub oil into your legs, bathe
your tired feet, squeeze

them until your tingles
shoot up my arm, I chew each toe

in turn until it is softened, bite
into your soles like a joint of pork,

you cannot help but giggle,
sir, I turn you over,

with my palms, rotate your temples, trace
the curves on your face, touching

yet not, three fingers inside your mouth, let you
suckle, baby,

from belly to breast, I massage
your chest

in concentric circles, pinch
your nipples, nibble gently, set my belly-dancer

tongue on to them, take your hands,
my love,

tie them above your head, with your belt,
I sit astride my steed,

take the reins, my flexible muscles
holding you in,

flexing like strong fists,
tighten and release,

teasing you, taming you, your eyes are shut,
you have died

and gone to Olympus, smiling,
I slap it off,

so hard my hand hurts,
your eyes shoot open like a dead man

dying,
I slap you again,

you feign amusement,
your eyes suggest *so this is slap and tickle*?

I take your riding crop, fold it,
lash your chest.

'Take that!' I hiss. 'How *dare* you humour me.
Who's the boss now?'

I ride you so hard I am becoming sore.
Forget

those stinking back-stabbers
in the senate in Rome, Severus,

those shit-stirrers, perfidious smilers,
has-beens, cunning

poisoners, ruthless young guns, arse-
lickers, mendacious gits,

wannabes – and your wife,
who won't play make-believe.

I know,
Who?
Who?
Who?
Who?

I demand with each merciless thrust.
'You *silly* girl,' you snicker, 'untie me now.'

I slap you again, but throw aside the whip,
for I have not the will, in truth,

to see you bleed.
'Outside!' I order, watch you struggle

to crawl
on your tied hands and knees, laughing

hysterically like a naughty child.
Is this so funny? I kick you hard in the ribs,

you collapse on your back,
when did anyone *ever* dare, my *imperator*?

I mount,
we are in mud, mud and more mud,

et caenum et caenum et plus caeni,
you are sprawled in it,

my legs have sunk
into it, my flattened hands

are imprinted on it,
rain pours down my back, over my head,

my nose, into my mouth, yours,
I gulp it in,

grab handfuls of mud, plaster your cheeks,
your chest,

in sludge,
you are helpless,

this is pure oestrus, sir,
we are mating

beasts,
with no history, no future

but my bloodline to continue.
I begin

riding my boy home.
'Who's the boss?'

He responds to my thrusts with such force
I almost fall off

him, he surges, he must surrender
before *I* break,

this friction will make me scream,
prematurely,

I stop, wait, letting his hardness
beg from inside, I act cold,

taunting.
'Don't stop now,' he panics.

'Who's the boss,' I repeat, folding my arms,
smirking.

'Please, Zuleika,'
'Say the magic words.'

'You are!'
'I am *what*?'

'You are –
my imperatrix, my canny dominatrix,

mistress of all you survey,'
he spews out,

a tad too arrogantly.
'Mmnn,' I reply,

'try saying it with more sincerity,
more humility, methinks.'

I move to get off him.
'No! You are boss,' he says urgently.

'Don't leave me now, come home
with me,

maman, take me home,'
he moans,

'take me home, maman,
I want to go home, home, home,'

please, Zuleika,
take me . . .'

I unbelt his hands,
his body spasms, he claws

my breasts with muddy fingers,
cries out, choking on a mouthful of rain,

he spumes
into me and we are all pulpa,

the swollen river
has become a torrent,

I hear it rushing past us,
later we bathe in it, I dip

your head
gently, rinse the mud from your curls,

rain showers us,
you clean my breasts

with wet hands,
make them shine again,

your weight holds out
against the current,

you hold me
so tight I do not fall,

we walk
back to the tent, me

leading you,
we dry each other off, gently,

with soft towels,
lie down together,

wrapped into ourselves,
our carriage is made of pure gold,

we sit on top of purple cushions,
this is our triumphal procession

into Rome.

Vivat Imperator Severus!
Vivat Imperator Severus!

Thousands are cheering
on the streets,

from windows, from the roofs of buildings,
hundreds of silver trumpets

are heralding your return,
after so long,

you have taken Scotland,
all the buildings and statues

are adorned,
with flowers and ribbons

wrapped around columns,
sandalwood burns in braziers,

the army is behind you,
dancers are ahead of you.

Bellissima! Bellissima!
they call out to your new bride.

We enter the Imperial Palace
on the Palatine Hill,

where we sleep
the sleep of newborns,

you hold me so tightly
I cannot move,

I am your life,
we will re-create each other,

we will call her
Claudia,

she will call you
Daddums.

I cannot hold out,
my body is erupting

like a volcano,
the sun inside me, lightning

striking me,
I am on fire,

I am riding a wave,
I grab the mud either side

to steady myself, but
it is slipping

through my fingers, I will
explode

into a billion fragments of sand,
into the rain, I throw

back my head
and howl.

X

WHEN YOU LEAST EXPECT

Hands pressed down on my jugular.
I woke up, struggling to breathe, coughing,

the walls closed in, there was no air.
Wild-eyed, I quickly dressed, flung a veil

over my head, rushed outside, was sucked
towards the vortex of the town,

but the Temple was eerily silent.
Where was the drone of invocations?

Stalls were abandoned in the streets, braziers
left unchecked, goods hung unguarded

outside shops, doorways opened on to empty
workshops, no hammers, no shouting

yet the air hummed with activity, as if
they'd only just left. I hurriedly

turned into Lombard Street, hordes
were swaying towards the Forum, poured out

of alleys, swept into the swell of excited voices.
I tried to decipher the babble, no one would stop.

The bell of the Basilica began to resound
Mortuus . . . in his sleep . . . Severus . . .

The whirl of colour swam on without me –
shoals of fish around a rock.

VALE, FAREWELL, MY LIBYAN

you
have
murdered me
you bastard

you have
died
at
York

ALBATROSS

Requiescat in pace,
there is no more war, soldier.

I rock myself into night
which is day,
and day
which is night,

I rise,
the room is spinning and I am flying,

I have wings,
my span is great,
I take flight.

THE LANGUAGE OF LOVE (III)

The sun is a gangrenous sore
oozing pus into the cesspit of the Thames;
when it has sunk
behind the mud flats of Southwark,
when I am indistinguishable from night,
I will swim to the ferryman,
sweet chariot of Charon,
coming for to carry me back
into oblivion,
to the waveless waters of my embryonic sac –
and as the waves make towards
the pebbled shore,
so will my minutes hasten towards my end,
leaving a crumpled pink frock,
and sling-backs.

ANIMULA VAGULA
(Little Soul Flitting Away)

Please, I want to go to Hades.
Just put a coin in my mouth
and send me home to Daddy.

My limbs rot inside my kid-leather curves,
dainty goatskin sandals lead me
across the cubiculum to my dresser,
my mind hobbles, my legs so light,
they defy gravity, almost.

A bone phoenix handle, a looking glass,
its wings hold up my silver polished world,
but I shift in and out of existence,
I cannot focus.

Hungry for air, my tissue absorbs my liquids.
Must breathe deeply
to survive; the stench of a decomposing corpse
is mine. My body accepts
the prison of bones, its decay.

I am only flesh and blood, Severus,
and you have staked my heart.

DOMUM DULCE DOMUM
(Home Sweet Home)

He sailed up the Thames, Felix the Great,
on a ship laden with amphorae of spices,

marble and fresh slaves from Palestine.
Severus had sent him to lead a trading

expedition to India, at the last minute,
he complained, RIP etc., but at his age

he was getting past all that gallivanting;
but wasn't he exsultatus to be home

with his so pulcherrima wife, especially
after all those beer-drinking Britannicos

on the east coast, stubbornly living
in mud huts and reeking of BO

as if they were still in the Bronze Age, I ask you.
'Londinium! You have grown on me,

as a child does on a parent,
after Roma, Neapolis, Alexandria,

Antioch, Carthage, Jerusalem –
you are the best city in the world!' he sang out,

flinging open the shutters on to the Walbrook
which passed to a sprinkle of rain below.

I noticed a full moon growing out
of his pudding-bowl haircut, and blue worms

wriggling in his even thinner calves.
He spun around: two more teeth had gone,

and the rest were a battered stone wall.
I *wanted* to smell juniper.

'Tonight we party!' He embraced me.
'Call Tranio! We will have jugglers,

acrobats, musicians, even poets, why not?
Invite the governor and all local notables

and right honourables, but first
to the baths in preparation for a feast

of culinary miracles and miraculous cunnilinctus.'
He winked, slapped my rump.

'My coming home present, mea delicia,'
then he disappeared outside

for a shit.

EXIT STRATAGEM

Valeria and Aemilia, my darling swine,
who could have predicted their betrayal?

You clothe and feed two stinking urchins
as if they were your own. You do *not* sell

them to a merchant from Europa
(for *plenty* baksheesh!). And your reward?

As soon as I left the house to go to Fish Street Hill
to select the choicest cod from the quay,

those evil-mongers poured poison into Felix's ears.
It was still morning when I returned, resolved

to put my desire on a boat and let it drown
in the infinite ocean surrounding our world.

As I walked in, those vixens rushed past me
without a glance or by-your-leave, ma'am.

And there stood Felix, facing Medusa, fisted
arms towards the sky as if in the denouement

of the ultima tragoedia.
'Husband?' I ventured, and he turned,

snarling like a rabid dog, and I realized
that on the perfumed bed of love

I had not cared about discovery
and in the torpor of my grief I had not thought

that my lover's protection would go with his life.
Felix asked no explanation, his mind

was as powerful as imperium and I
was some poor sod in a loincloth in Judaea.

'I, Felix Aurelius Lucius, created a lady
out of a sewer rat and your thanks?

I am the laughing stock of this town.
I trusted you and I have been *utterly* humiliated.'

I was banished to my cubiculum
and locked in.

THE PRICE YOU PAY, MY BEAUTIFUL WIFE

Bread and cheese, baked eggs,
fish in spicy sauces; I pondered jumping

into the Walbrook, but where would I go?
Dad would as soon as kill me, I could

not involve the girls, for Felix would hunt
me down and make them pay, and to leave

the city wall was to risk unknown horrors.
Was my punishment to come?

A husband could do what he liked
and many an errant wife ended up

in an unmarked grave outside the city walls.
I did not scream, though, hammering

on the door for forgiveness,
but accepted what was due.

I had relished a death so sweet that nothing
would ever match it again;

nascentes morimur, from the moment
of being born, we die, after all.

I had lived my life.

VADE IN PACE
(Go in Peace)

When the door was unbolted,
my husband had gone, off to attend

the emperor's wake in York, Tranio said,
lowering his gaze. Had I paid my dues?

Those barbarian bitches had gone too.
This was ominous. Another week passed.

I was not allowed out of the house, I wandered
from room to room and only

when I was too weak to sit up did I find out
it was not despair sapping my energy

but arsenicum hidden in spicy sauces.
My home had become my mausoleum.

I asked for Alba and Venus: Tranio refused.
'I have my orders, miss.'

'Of course you owe *me* nothing. Not even a *wife*.
And by the way, it is madam to you.'

But I could not be angry with him, in truth.
Because he had not spilled the beans,

as he should have, he was implicated.
He had to survive. I was a goner anyway.

This time he followed Felix's instructions
as loyally as every good slave should.

What was it? So much each day, send word
when the little whore has snuffed it?

Another husband might have been proud
that the emperor had picked his wife

out of the millions queuing worldwide.
He will regret it, when he calms down,

after weeks, months, even years.
But he'll never be able to speak of it,

and it will rot like an incurable ulcer
festering inside his stomach.

It was the last days of summer, the sun
had become a faltering heart beat,

I lay down on a couch in the atrium,
I had lost the ability to walk.

I opened my eyes and saw Alba enter
through the main doorway. Alba.

Dear, dear Alba. She rushed over.
'Tranio sent for me. He's told me! The fuckwit!

I'll kill that grunting hog.
How long have you been like this?

No matter. Come, I'm taking you *with*.'
She tried to pull me up by my arms,

but I resisted. 'No, Alba. It's fate.'
'Oh, sod fucking fate, while we live, let us *live*!'

'No! It's too late now anyway.'
'I told you it would come to no good.

I will kill that grotesque bastard Felix. I *will.*'
Rage and sorrow competed to contort

the features on her face, neither winning.
'I'm dead anyway. Can't you see?

I was given life, then it was taken away,
the actual act of dying is mere procedure.

It's just breath now, a rain cloud on my chest,
and that's getting harder to push out.'

'Don't be so heroic, Zuleika. I can't stand it.'
'And don't be so dramatic, Alba.

This isn't a Greek tragoedia, though
it could be mistaken for one.'

'Life's so unfair, Zee.'
I was silent, then,

'Innit.'
'I can't imagine life without you.'

'Don't start whining. Just sit with me awhile,
and then go home, and remember me.'

It was all I allowed myself to think of now –
the first ten years, to remember

the married years, or the memory
of my euphoric summer of love,

felt like flinging myself atop a raging fire.
She sat down on the couch, held my hands,

tears flowing freely down cheeks brutalized
by bursting blood vessels.

'This shouldn't have happened, Zeeks.
This is unbearable, unbelievable, un –'

'You've been my *best* friend, Albs.'
'I know.'

'You're wonderful in spite of your faults.'
'I know.'

'What's going to become of you, eh?
You'll get VD one of these days. You can't

screw around for ever. You need to focus.'
'What, and end up like you?'

'Out of order, Albs. Bit below the purse-pouch.'
'Sorry, Zee! Sorry! Sorry! It's still sinking in.'

'There's no time for us to bicker. Answer me.'
'I'll be in search of more adventures, as usual.

I've me eye on someone, a lawyer this time.
I took V's hint. Omnipotent stallholders?'

She was completely beyond redemption, my Alba,
I hoped the gods would treat her gently.

'But this isn't about me, Zuleika, it's about you.'
'Which means it's about both of us.

Where is Venus the Penis?'
'Incommunicado. Can you believe it,

she's actually taken Big P to meet
her old boy and girl in deepest Camulodunum.

She'll be devastated. Absolutely gutted.'
'Tell her for me she's a silly old tart,

that I hope they're very happy together,
and have lots of hermaphrodite kiddies

with ginger dreadlocks and hendecasyllables
pouring out of their freckled little arses.'

'I will.' Her expression read – how can you
be funny at a time like this? How could I not?

I'd gone from my zenith to my nadir,
all in two short weeks. It was hysterical.

'Felix isn't a bad man, you know.
He's the person he was brought up to be,

like all of us, even Venus, except
he did it with less imagination than most.

The only original thing he did was to wed
below his class, even then he hid me away.

He never knew me, you know, never knew
the wild child who would want more,

never once asked, "What do *you* want?"'
'Zuleika, don't make excuses for that gargoyle.'

'There are drops of clarity,
Poison does that to you.
Imminent death allows the birth
Of new perspectives.
When there is nothing left to lose,
For everything is lost,
Truth is a most welcome friend.

That's my swan song, I think
it's the only decent thing I've ever written.

I've called it "Mors Certa, Hora Incerta",
"Death Certain, Hour Uncertain".

Was I a plaything for Severus, do you think?'
It had been bugging me. The refrain.

'What? With all the attention he paid you?
Trips out, treats, quality time alone? *Hardly!*'

'You're right. I was of great comfort to him,
and vicky versa. Will you bury me, Alba?

You know Felix has no intention, nor The Pops.'
'Don't be so morbid.'

'I'm being pragmatic. Felix will chuck me out
as carrion, with a banner above my head:

I curse Zuleika and her life and mind
and memory and liver and lungs mixed up
together; thus may she be condemned
to pouring water into bottomless jars for ever.

Will you do it?'
'You know I will. 'Course I will.'

'Dress me in my violet damask dalmatica
with gold thread, it's laid out on my bed.

Severus sent for the material from the best
workshop in Syria, got a one-off made for me.

I wonder if they recognize designer labels
where I'm going? Get my hair

done in beautiful elaborate braids. Marcia'll do it,
she's head stylist at Kinky Girls on Cornhill.

I want a pillow of the sweetest smelling
bay leaves and a scallop-shell design

on the lid of my coffin so that my journey
is safe, oh, and don't forget my jet afro pick,

tweezers and especially my nail file –
I don't want to look a state when I arrive.

Can you imagine, gorgon's nails
and matted hair. Got that?'

'Right you are, ma'am,' she said, saluting.
'And I want to be buried at the cemetery

in Spitalfields, not some nondescript
out-of-town site for the plebs, get the money

off Cato or Venus. And last but not least,
a tombstone, with this inscription:

To the spirits of the departed
And the memory of our pal Zuleika,
Who in her final summer
Lived a life fuller than any other.'

We sat there. Words? What words?
'I wanted to be important, Albs.'

'You're important to me. We're sisters.'
'That's not the same, though, is it?

I wanted to be a great poet or mosaicist
or something. I'd have made a good empress.'

'The best!'
'It was all that bloody schooling that did it.

Theodorus going on about the greats for years
made me want to be a great myself.

Now it's too late. I'm still only eighteen.
It's my nineteenth birthday next week.

Light a candle for me. Now go home!
Your miserable face is making this worse.

Go home.'

EPILOGUE

VIVAT ZULEIKA

It is you I have found to wear, Zuleika,
lying in a panel of summer,
your golden couch moved into the atrium
to feed your skin, for the last time.

I enter quietly from Watling Court,
the pounding bass and horns of the City's
square mile, suspended. Between
two columns, your couch faces a pool

fed by the aching stone mouth of Medusa.
A cloud chills you in its shadow
of passing – Zuleika moritura est.
Now is the time. I glide to where you lie,

look upon your pink robes, ruched,
décolleté, a mild stir with each tired breath,
pronounced mould of your face, obsidian
with light and sweat, so tranquilla

in your moment of leaving. I slip
into your skin, our chest stills, drains
to charcoal. You have expired, Zuleika,
and I will know you, from the inside.

ACKNOWLEDGEMENTS

My heartfelt thanks to my editors, Caroline White at Viking, USA, and Simon Prosser at Penguin, UK, for their great enthusiasm and commitment to this book; to my copy editor, Donna Poppy, and the team at Penguin; my agents Hannah Griffiths at Curtis Brown and Emma Parry in New York; my tour manager, Melanie Abraham of Renaissance One; the Museum of London, especially Chandan Mahal and the Interpretation Unit, and the curator Jenny Hall; the Poetry Society for my residency at the Museum; the Arts Council of England for my Writers' Award 2000; the British Council for numerous opportunities to tour abroad; the following people for acts of support: Ruth Borthwick, Colin Channer, Kwame Dawes, Catriona Ferguson, Brendan Griggs, Mel Jennings, Helen Swords and Jacob Ross; Victoria Evaristo and Patricia St. Hilaire for keeping me sane(r) through endless telephone conversations; and to the historian Peter Fryer, author of the truly groundbreaking book *Staying Power: The History of Black People in Britain*, where I first learnt that Africans had lived in Britain during the Roman occupation nearly eighteen hundred years ago.

Printed in the United States
by Baker & Taylor Publisher Services